Under
the
influence

W. E. BUTTERWORTH

Under the influence

FOUR WINDS PRESS
NEW YORK

LIBRARY OF CONGRESS CATALOGING IN PUBLICATION DATA

Buterworth, William E
  Under the influence.

  SUMMARY: As their friendship deepens, Allan realizes that Keith is an
alcoholic whose behavior jeopardizes the well-being of himself and
others.
  [1. Alcoholics — Fiction. 2. Friendship — Fiction] I. Title.
PZ7.B9825Un [Fic.] 78-22127
ISBN 0-590-07465-2

PUBLISHED BY FOUR WINDS PRESS
A DIVISION OF SCHOLASTIC MAGAZINES, INC., NEW YORK, N.Y.
COPYRIGHT © 1979 BY W. E. BUTTERWORTH
ALL RIGHTS RESERVED
PRINTED IN THE UNITED STATES OF AMERICA
LIBRARY OF CONGRESS CATALOG CARD NUMBER: 78-22127
2 3 4 5 83 82 81 80

Under
the
influence

CHAPTER 1

It never happened at Bartram High, at least so far as I know, and I think the kids would have talked about it if it had. Officially it never happened at Richard Stockton High School either, although I was there when it did. That's how I met Keith Stevens.

What I'm talking about is punching an assistant football coach in the mouth. It was the second day of fall practice for the Stockton Patriots. I was a senior, and I had just transferred to Stockton. Keith had just transferred too, but the circumstances were a little different.

We had both played varsity ball, me at Bartram High in the

city, and Keith at a private school he'd gone to in New England. Both of us had been halfbacks, and we were trying out for the same position at Stockton. The guys we were competing against had played for the Patriots (or sat on the bench) the year before. They had ended the season with the idea that this year they would be the halfbacks. They weren't exactly happy with the idea that they might be knocked out of that by two newcomers.

They know about me. I'd been a halfback, as I said, at Bartram, and we had played and beaten Stockton. They didn't know about Keith, but it was apparent even on the first day of practice that Keith was quite a football player. He was better than I was, and I was better than the guys who saw that their jobs were in danger.

I came from a football family. My father played football for Bartram, and so did both my brothers. One of the real reasons I hated moving out to Springview from the city was that I wouldn't get to play for Bartram in my last year of high school.

I don't want to be misunderstood when I say we were pretty good football players. There was no chance at all that some scout for a college team would be coming around waving a full scholarship at us. We were good compared to the competition because the competition wasn't good at all. One of the two games Bartram had won was against Stockton. The other game we won was against Central, where football was regarded almost as a joke.

When I look back now on what happened, I think I understand it. For one thing I don't think the coaches where Keith had gone to school talked to their players the way Mr. Jozak talked to the players at Stockton. Let's face it, some of the language coaches use when they're excited isn't the sort of language you normally use.

I'm not a prude. When your father and two brothers are cops, you don't end up a prude. I knew all the words, and while I didn't particularly like having some of them used on me, they didn't make me either break out in tears or take a poke at the assistant coach.

That's one thing. For another I really think that Mr. Jozak had already realized that Keith Stevens was a better football player than the rest of us, and that he would be a halfback. He was leaning over backward, sort of, to show that Keith wasn't getting any special treatment. The way he did that was by leaning on him pretty hard. I'd had some experience in getting leaned on. I had, as I said, two brothers. The worst thing you can do when someone is leaning on you is to let him see that he's getting to you. The technique is to ignore it, if you can.

I was ignoring both Mr. Jozak and the two guys whose jobs we were about to take away. I could see that they were getting to Keith, but even in the short time I'd known him (we had the same homeroom and English IV, From Beowulf to Thomas Hardy, together), I had seen that he was a pretty smooth character. I was as surprised as anybody when he belted Mr. Jozak.

The way you get at people is to point out how they're different. Keith was different from the other guys in two ways. First of all he was hardly what you would call good looking. He looked like a gorilla. He had a square head, a flat nose, not much of a neck, long arms, and short legs. Let's face it. A lot of football players look like that. But what made it sort of stand out with Keith was the way he talked. His accent, the way he pronounced words, was different. He used a lot of big words, and coming from someone who looked the way he did, this made him stand out, too. Mr. Jozak had picked up on this and begun to mimic the way he talked.

What happened exactly was this. We were doing rushing practice. There's a big leather bag filled with sand and sawdust suspended from a rope. The guys got in a line, and then when Mr. Jozak said "hup!" or something like that, they rushed the bag, hitting it with their shoulders. I was steadying the bag so that it would present a heavier target. That's why I was there and saw and heard exactly what happened.

When Mr. Jozak saw that I was back in place after the last guy had hit the bag, he called "hup!" and Keith rushed it. He gave it a good belt. I was holding it, and I know.

When Keith straightened up, he looked at Mr. Jozak. Mr. Jozak was looking at him with scorn on his face. Then he put his right arm up in the air, let the wrist dangle, scratched his armpit with the other hand, and said, "Come on, King Kong, you can do better than that." There was no mistaking what he meant. Keith was a dumb ape.

"What do you mean by that?" Keith asked, and I saw he was white in the face.

"You know exactly what I mean, Stevens," Mr. Jozak said. "This is tackle, Stevens, *tackle!* Try hitting it again. If you do it right, maybe I'll give you a banana."

"And what is that supposed to imply?" Keith asked, in his precise (I guess the word is *cultured*) accent. "That and the armpit scratching?"

"What do you think I meant to *imply*?" Mr. Jozak said, mimicking him. "I meant that on this team even a big ape is expected to follow simple instructions."

"Don't call me an ape again," Keith said. "I find it offensive."

"Oh, pardon me," Mr. Jozak said. "The last thing in the world I would want to do is offend you."

"And I don't think your sarcasm is at all amusing," Keith said.

"I'm not trying to be amusing. I take football very seriously," Mr. Jozak said. He walked up to Keith and they glowered at each other a minute. Then Mr. Jozak did the ape-scratching-his-armpit routine again. "Got it, Apeman?"

Keith hit him. It was over almost before I saw it coming. Keith just cocked his right hand back, made a fist, and belted Mr. Jozak in the mouth. He connected, too. There was a splat noise, and Mr. Jozak went sailing backward. His mouth started to bleed almost immediately.

For a second nobody moved. Then the guys in line, including the two guys who had been counting on making halfback, grabbed Keith. I don't think they had time to plan what they did to him. It just happened. Anyway what happened was that two guys grabbed him, and a third guy started hitting him in the stomach.

He hit him three, four times before I came around from behind the bag and laid one on him. His mouth must have been open when I hit him, for there was a sharp pain on my fingers, and when I looked at my hand, I saw that it was bleeding.

Things got a little confused after that, and the next thing I remember is two guys holding me and the face of Coach Ramsey himself, actually white he was so mad, shouting at me to go to the locker room and wait for him there.

It was a long walk from where this had all happened, down by the south goal, to the tunnel through the grandstands which led to the locker room. Keith walked in a moment after I did, but neither of us said anything until we were inside the showers.

"That was my scrap," Keith finally said, as I turned the water off and stepped out of the stall. "But thanks for the help." I didn't reply. I don't know whether I was scared or still angry, but there didn't seem to be much to say. I knew I was in trouble, and it was that bad kind of trouble, when you know you would do the same thing again.

Then he saw my hand.

"You must have hit him in the teeth," he said matter-of-factly. "You'd better do something about that. Human teeth punctures are the most dangerous of all."

"How about shark bites?" I heard myself saying. We looked at each other, and suddenly it was funny. Or we thought it was funny. We were probably both almost hysterical, but anyway we laughed.

I wrapped a towel around my middle and we went to the first-aid cabinet in the locker room. It was locked. It was sort of a symbolic little lock, stuck through the loop of a small hasp.

"That figures," Keith said, and shrugged his shoulders and reached up and twisted it off. "Now they can get me for breaking and entering as well as assault with intent to do bodily harm," Keith said. "I should be eligible for parole by 1980."

He took a bottle of Merthiolate from the cabinet, and then after thinking about it, a bottle of hydrogen peroxide. He took my arm and marched me to a basin.

"Fear not young man," he said. "Place your faith in Doctor Stevens."

He poured the peroxide over the gouge in my fingers. It stung and looked terrible. The peroxide bubbled.

"Be a big boy and don't cry, and you get an all-day sucker," he said.

"How come, if it was your fight, I get to bleed?" I asked.

"Because I'm smarter than you are, obviously," he said.

We waited until the peroxide stopped bubbling, and then he poured Merthiolate on my fingers.

"You'll live," he said. "You will probably have to go through life known as Three Fingers . . . what's your name?"

"Corelli," I said.

"As Three Fingers Corelli," Keith went on, "whose promising career as a flamenco guitar player was nipped in the bud in a brawl."

Coach Ramsey came in then. He marched up to us, grabbed my hand, and examined the fingers.

"You'd better see a doctor," he said, disgust in his voice. "What's the matter with you, anyway?"

"He has this sense of fair play for the underdog," Keith said. "Whenever he sees three guys beating up on one guy, he has to play D'Artagnan and rush to the rescue."

Coach Ramsey just looked at him.

"D'Artagnan," Keith repeated. "One of the characters in *The Three Musketeers*."

"For somebody up to his neck in serious trouble," Coach Ramsey said, "you've got a big mouth."

"I don't have a big mouth," Keith said. "You should be talking to Mr. Jozak."

"You'll be lucky if Mr. Jozak doesn't press charges," Coach Ramsey said.

"I'll plead justifiable provocation," Keith said. "I told him to knock it off."

"Knock what off?"

"I don't like people reminding me I look like an ape," Keith said.

"You're not trying to tell me Mr. Jozak said anything like that?"

"That's exactly what I'm saying," Keith said.

"You're obviously mistaken," the coach said.

"I might have been mistaken when he scratched his armpit," Keith said, "but there was no mistaking what he meant when he offered me a banana. And he called me 'Apeman,' the *second* time he scratched his armpit."

"I don't believe you," the coach said.

"I saw it all, Coach," I said. "That's exactly what happened."

"I warned him," Keith said. "I told him I found it offensive. And then he did it again."

"Even if something like that happened, that didn't give you the right to punch him," the coach said. He was no longer quite as righteous as he had been, but I knew that he would still stand by Mr. Jozak. He turned to me. "And what gave you the right to hit Dowson? You loosened two of his teeth."

"Two guys were holding me while Dowson hit me," Keith said. "That's when Corelli hit him."

"That's not the way they tell it," the coach said. "The way I heard it, after you hit Mr. Jozak they tried to hold you to keep you from hitting him again, and then your pal jumped in."

"I only hit him once," Keith said. "Once was enough. Then his fan club jumped me."

"I don't like your attitude, Stevens," Coach Ramsey said. "You don't seem at all sorry about any of this."

"The only thing I'm sorry about is that Corelli cut his hand," Keith said.

"You realize, of course, that this ends any chance either of you had to play ball?" Coach Ramsey said.

"Why's that?" Keith asked.

"There's no place on any team of mine for a couple of brawlers," Coach Ramsey said.

"What about those three brawlers who ganged up on me?" Keith asked.

"The point is, Stevens, that you started it," the coach said.

"*I* started it?" Keith responded incredulously.

"You started it, and you're responsible for everything that came out of it," the coach said. "Under the circumstances I think I can talk Mr. Jozak into not going to the principal or the police, but you're through with the team as of right now."

Keith got white in the face again, and for a second I thought he might take a poke at the coach, but he didn't.

"Look," he said, "Corelli didn't start anything. There's no reason to throw him off the team."

"If you're off the team," I heard myself saying, "so am I."

"And that's the way it's going to be," the coach said. "Turn in your equipment."

"Now wait a minute," Keith said. "Just a second."

"Well?"

"So far as I'm concerned, there's wrong on both sides. I suppose I shouldn't have hit Jozak, but—"

"You *suppose* you shouldn't have hit a member of the faculty?" Coach Ramsey said sarcastically.

"And I *know* that a *member of the faculty* isn't supposed to go calling students dumb apes," Keith said.

"So?"

"I don't really mind getting thrown off your team," Keith said, "but I don't want to have to work up a sweat playing volleyball with the sick, lame, and lazy."

I knew what he meant by that. If you were out for football, you were excused from regular physical education classes. I don't suppose I'd gone to ten regular PE classes since I'd been in high school. I was excused in the fall because I had junior varsity, and then varsity football. Then for the month or six weeks before baseball started I'd always gone out for track, fooling around with the hammer and discus and javelin. I hadn't been much of a track jock, but it was sort of a fringe benefit for playing ball. You were given a free ride so you didn't have to play volleyball with, as Keith had put it, the sick, lame, and lazy, which is the way the football and baseball players thought of the guys who didn't go out for varsity sports.

Now that Keith had brought it up, I quickly saw that the price I was going to pay for losing my temper was joining the regular phys. ed. classes. I didn't like the idea for a couple of reasons. For one thing, what it would look like was that we hadn't been good enough to make the team. That just wasn't so.

I looked at the coach. Keith had upset him. It wasn't hard to figure out what he was thinking. He wasn't used to being challenged by a student, but he realized that Keith was right. Mr. Jozak had been as wrong as Keith had been. Keith could raise a large stink about being abused by Mr. Jozak. On the other hand making us go to the regular phys. ed. classes wasn't all that important. The idea was to give the guys who weren't naturally athletic some exercise. Keith and I didn't need that, and the coach knew it.

Still, I figured, waiting for him to speak, rules are rules and coaches have to support assistant coaches, and more important, students don't go around bargaining with, or threatening (even if the threat wasn't spoken out loud), football coaches.

"Okay," the coach said. "You're excused from PE through the football season. I'll work it out somehow."

Keith had won. I was surprised. But it wasn't a pleasant victory. I wished the whole thing hadn't happened. I had to remind myself that Keith really hadn't started it. Mr. Jozak should have known better than to push him that hard.

The coach walked out of the locker room. We got dressed without saying anything.

"Hey," Keith said, as we dumped all our gear on the counter of the equipment room. "I'm sorry, Corelli. I mean it. This cost you a lot more than it cost me."

"Forget it," I said. "I wasn't that wild about playing for Stockton anyway." That wasn't exactly true, but it wasn't all a lie, either.

"You transferred in too, didn't you?" he asked, and I nodded. "From where?"

"Bartram," I said. "We beat Stockton last year."

"Well since there's no sense crying over spilt milk, as I always say, let's go get a beer."

"Where are we going to do that?" I asked.

"At my house," he said. "My mother will be so relieved that I'm not going to have my handsome profile smashed and battered in this vulgar and brutal game that we could probably have champagne. Except I don't like champagne. Booze and beer is all."

We walked out of the stadium. Faintly I could hear the noise of practice on the field. It didn't seem right somehow that practice should be going on. But it would be, of course. There would be football. And they didn't need us. We wouldn't even be missed.

It occurred to me that for the first time since I'd been a freshman, I wasn't part of the team. I was an ex-football player. I was outside. It was a very strange feeling. I felt sort of light-headed. And in the pit of my stomach I felt a little lost, even a little sick.

CHAPTER 2

Keith's car surprised me. I was never crazy about cars the way some guys are, but I was impressed with a Mercedes. It was a silver-gray 280 SE, a lot of car.

"That's quite a set of wheels," I said.

"It was my father's," Keith said, as he put the key in the ignition.

"Was?"

"He died—dropped dead of a heart attack—in August," Keith said.

"I'm sorry," I said.

"Yeah," he said. "So'm I. He was a good guy, as fathers go."

We headed up Whitman Avenue and after a while he turned to me and asked, "What about your father?"

"What about him?"

"Good guy?"

"Yeah," I said. It was true. "Me getting the heave-ho is going to make his whole day."

"Trouble?"

"Nothing serious," I said.

"What's he do?"

"He's a cop," I said.

"Oh?" Keith said. What I said wasn't true, or at least it wasn't the whole truth.

"Actually, he's the chief of police," I said.

"Oh?" Keith said, and now he was fascinated.

"That's how come I'm here," I said. "He used to be on the force in Newark, but then they offered him chief here, and we moved."

"What kind of a cop?" he asked. "In Newark, I mean."

"He was chief of detectives," I said.

"And do you want to be a cop when you grow up?" Keith asked. The "when you grow up" part was said mockingly.

"Maybe," I said. "Probably. It runs in the family. My grandfather was on the force. My brothers are both cops."

"Fascinating," he said.

"It's a job," I said. I remembered that my father was always saying that.

"Rude question: More money here? Is that why he moved?"

"I guess," I said. "That and the idea that the hours would be better."

"My father was a stockbroker," Keith said. "Nothing at all interesting. Unless you're interested in making money."

"And you're not?"

"I don't know," he said.

"My mother's dead," I offered.

"That makes us semi-orphans, I suppose," he said. "How long ago?"

"When I was six," I said. "My Aunt Rose takes care of us."

"Maybe we can work something out between your old man and my mother," he said.

I didn't think that was especially funny, and I had the feeling that he realized it wasn't. He didn't say anything else at all until we had ridden just about all the way up Whitman Avenue, and then turned off onto one of the streets which run off it. The sign said "Mountain Brook Drive."

The house matched the car. There was also another Mercedes— a yellow coupe—and a Ford station wagon. The station wagon was on one side of the garage, and the coupe was sitting on the wide, turn-around driveway.

We got out of the car.

"You know," he said, "I'll bet *El Coacho* remembered who your old man is."

"What do you mean?"

"I didn't really think I was going to get away with getting out of phys. ed.," Keith said.

"Neither did I," I said.

"I was trying to figure out why. Now I know. The fuzz wouldn't ignore the chief's son."

"Knock off that 'fuzz' business, okay?" I said. I was annoyed with him.

"Sorry," he said. "No offense intended, Corelli."

"And knock off the Corelli too, will you?"

"Sensitive about that, too? Because it sounds Italian?"

"No, because you're not Mr. Jozak, and I can tell you when I don't like being called by my last name, like I'm in the army, or in jail."

"Okay. What's your first name?"

"Al."

"Short for Alphonse, as in Capone?" he said, wearing a large smile.

"Short for Allan," I said. "You bigoted wasp."

"Well now that's settled and out of the way, come on, Mafioso, and we'll guzzle some bootleg booze."

We walked into the garage, but instead of entering the house Keith led me down a passageway that opened into the basement. Except it really wasn't a basement. The house sat on the side of the mountain (I suppose in Arizona or Wyoming they'd call it a "hill," but here in Jersey we call it a mountain), and what would have been a basement in a house built on flatland was just another level of the house here.

Wide, curtained, plate-glass windows where one basement wall would normally have been gave a view of Springview at the bottom of the mountain, and further away you could see Newark. Probably, I thought, on a clear day you could see all the way to New York.

Set against the opposite wall of the room was a bar. There were a dozen or more bottles of different kinds of whiskey, and even rows of glasses stacked on glass shelves like a bar. The only thing missing was a cash register. There was even a beer tap.

The room was furnished with yellow wicker furniture. There were four or five armchairs, two couches, two large tables, and maybe half a dozen small ones. A large color television was set against the wall with the windows, so if you got bored with the boob tube, you could look out on the lights below.

"Very nice," I said. What I was thinking was that it must be nice to be rich. I guess I was a little embarrassed because the next thing I knew I heard myself asking, "Does that thing work?" I was pointing at the beer tap.

"Only when there's a party," Keith said matter-of-factly. "Otherwise the beer—they deliver it in what they call a half-keg—goes stale." He walked behind the bar, bent over, and came up with two bottles of beer.

"Do you want a glass," Keith asked, "or do you believe, as I do, that it tastes better from the bottle?"

"From the bottle's fine," I said.

He twisted the caps off and handed me a bottle.

"Here's to us," he said. "We who play football not wisely, but too well."

We clinked the bottles.

"You know," Keith said, as he lowered himself into a chair beside a cabinet holding a stereo, "I really am sorry."

"You really shouldn't have hit him," I said.

"Oh, yes I should have," he said. "I don't regret that at all. What I'm sorry about is getting thrown off the team. Mostly I'm sorry that I got you thrown off. But also that I got thrown off. Now I'll never know whether or not I was really any good at it."

"What do you mean by that?"

"Well, at good ol' Saint Matt's, which is where I used to go to school, if you had the customary number of arms and legs, could hear thunder and see lightning, and weighed anything more than 150 pounds, you played football. Anybody as big as I am who didn't keep dropping the ball got to be a star. It was going to be different at Stockton."

"You'd have done all right," I said. "I think that's the real reason Jozak was leaning on you. You were better than the guys on last year's squad, and he could see it."

"From you that's a compliment," Keith said. "I will now blush modestly."

I took a pull at my bottle of beer.

"You ready for another?" Keith asked. I was really surprised to see that his was all gone. He'd really chug-a-lugged it.

"No," I said. "I just got started."

He returned to the bar and got himself another bottle of beer.

"I just had another unpleasant thought," he said, as he sat down again.

"What's that?"

"Now that I am an ex-football hero, where am I going to find adoring females?"

"Try cruising up and down Wilson Avenue in that Mercedes," I said. "That'll give you a little class. After all you can't ride a halfback to the movies."

There was the sound of high heels coming down wooden stairs. Keith looked past the bar, and I followed his eyes. A woman came into the room. She looked at first glance a lot younger than she looked a moment later. She had blond hair and was wearing a sweater and slacks.

"I thought I heard you come in," she said.

Keith waved a hand at her, "Mother, say hello to Allan Corelli."

I got up and shook the hand she put out to me.

"Hello, Allan," she said. "From your size I'd guess that you're another football player. Right?"

"Not quite, Mother," Keith said.

"I beg your pardon?"

"You are looking at two ex-football heroes," Keith said.

"You didn't make the team?" she asked. "Oh, I'm sorry for you, dear. But—"

"On the other hand, right?"

"I am sorry," she said.

"We were thrown off," Keith said.

"Thrown off?"

"You don't really want to hear the sordid details, do you?"

"I think I'd better hear them," she said.

"Cutting a long and dull story short, there was a fight," Keith said.

"Oh, Keith!"

"In which your fragile son was being assaulted by three big bad boys," he went on. "Whereupon D'Artagnan here jumped into the fray."

"And?"

"We won," Keith said. "That was just before they threw us both off the team."

"What was the fight about?"

"Certain offensive language was used, language which I dare not repeat in front of delicate female ears," Keith said. "When an apology was not forthcoming, I did what I said I was going to do. And, as they say, the battle was joined."

"Oh, Keith!" his mother said. "That's awful! I'm so sorry."

"Which explains why Allan wears that badge of honor on his paw," Keith said, "and why we sit here crying into our beer, our heads both bloodied and bowed."

Mrs. Stevens came to me.

"You hurt your hand, Allan?" she asked, and grabbed it before I knew what she was doing and pulled the bandage off. She might look like somebody's girl friend, I thought, but she had the instincts of a mother.

"Oh, that's nasty looking!" she said. She pulled me toward the bar.

"You should see the other guy," Keith said.

"There's a first-aid kit in the laundry," Mrs. Stevens said. "Get it, Keith."

"It's all right, Mrs. Stevens," I said. "Keith put peroxide and Merthiolate on it."

"You can never be too careful about cuts," she said firmly. She turned to Keith. "Go get the first-aid kit!"

"Yes, ma'am," he said. "Your wish is my command."

As he passed us, he put the second bottle of beer into a case under the bar. He really had a thirst, I thought.

"I don't mean to embarrass you, Allan," Mrs. Stevens said, "but do your parents permit you to drink?"

"Yes, ma'am," I said. I had never really thought about it quite that way before. I'm three-quarters Italian and a quarter Scotch. Italians drink wine, and I'd been given a glass of wine with meals as long as I could remember. And there was generally beer around the house, too. There was whiskey also, but no one in the family was really a whiskey drinker. My father might pour himself a drink every once in a while, and so did my brothers, Larry —Lawrence—who was a harness sergeant working municipal court, and Paul, who had just been transferred, a third-grade detective at twenty-four, to burglary after two years as a plainclothesman and as a narc on vice.

So far as they're concerned, and that meant me too, someone who "drank" was somebody who got drunk. None of us drank. But that wasn't what Mrs. Stevens was asking. She was asking if my father would object to me drinking a beer, and the answer to that was no. In that sense I was "permitted to drink." Not in what he called a "gin mill" of course, but like this in somebody's house.

Keith returned with a first-aid kit. Mrs. Stevens did the same thing to my fingers that Keith had done. She put antiseptic on the cut, using a stick with a ball of cotton on the end, instead of pouring peroxide from a bottle, and then she bandaged it, much more neatly than Keith.

"There," she said, giving me my hand back.

"Thank you," I said.

"Is there going to be any trouble about all this?" she asked, looking at me instead of at Keith. "With the school? Or with the police?"

"I handled the school with my usual finesse," Keith replied. "And we have no worries with the cops, none at all."

"How's that?"

"You have just bandaged the hand of the son of the chief of police," Keith said.

"Oh!" Mrs. Stevens said. "Of course. I should have connected the names. I met your father. He spoke to the League of Women Voters a week or two ago."

"Yes, ma'am," I said.

"Can you stay for supper, Allan? We're going to do something simple like broiled chicken, and we'd love to have you."

"Not tonight," I said. "Thank you. I'll take a rain check. But I have to be going."

"Well, finish your beer first," she said.

"Thank you," I said. I saw Keith dip into the cooler and come up with another beer.

"How many is that for you, young man?" his mother asked.

"Let me see," he replied. "Eight or nine. Maybe ten."

"Just be careful, dear," she said. She smiled at me, told me to come again, and left us alone.

Keith watched her go, and then he looked at me.

"I feel sorry as hell for her," he said. "She and my father got along pretty good. That doesn't often happen from what I've seen."

"She's very nice," I said.

"For a mother, she's first class," he said.

I finished my beer, and then we got back into the gray Mercedes and Keith drove me home.

"Right on my way," he said. "I drove past there this morning."

"One of the reasons my father bought this house," I said, "is because I could walk to school."

"I'll pick you up in the morning," he said, as he stopped the car. "We social pariahs must stick together."

"Come on in," I said. "My father's home. I can tell by the car with all the funny aerials on it."

"Okay," he said, and followed me in.

When I pushed open the door, the smell of food flooded us. My father was in the foyer, standing up by the telephone. He had his hand on his hip, unconsciously pushing the jacket away from the .38 Smith & Wesson snub-nose he carried in a holster which fit between the waistband of his trousers and his shirt.

He waved at me and grimaced at the telephone, and signaled for us to go into the living room. He gave Keith quite a going over with his eyes. I wondered if it were because Keith were with me, or whether he did this to everybody. In a moment he came into the living room.

"We're about to go Hollywood," he said.

"Huh?"

"Unlisted number," he said. "That did it. I'm not going to have every hysterical woman in Springview calling me at home."

"Dad, this is Keith Stevens," I said.

"How are you, Keith?" my father said.

"How do you do, sir?" Keith said politely. "Do I call you Chief?"

"Mr. Corelli will do fine," my father said. "I take off the badge when I walk through the door."

"That way," I said, "he doesn't have to warn me of my rights, or be careful about the rules of evidence. He can function like any other father."

"We have a simple rule that brings harmony to our happy home, Keith," my father said. "Whenever Tiny here talks back, or acts fresh, I let him have it with a blackjack."

"He's not kidding," I said. "He's worn out three blackjacks that way."

"Ordinarily, Keith," my father said, "we love to feed people, and we'd ask you to stay for supper. We'd *expect* you to stay for supper. But there's a special family thing tonight."

"I couldn't stay anyway, thank you," Keith said. "My mother's waiting for me at home. But thank you."

"Next time," my father said. He and Keith shook hands.

"I'll pick you up in the morning," Keith said to me.

"Great," I said. "See you."

We watched him walk out the door, and then I saw my father was looking at me. There was curiosity in his eyes.

"What happened to your hand?" he asked.

"Get out the blackjack," I said.

"What did you do?"

"I got thrown off the football team," I said.

"For what?"

"Fighting," I said. I realized my voice wasn't very firm.

"*Fighting?*" My father replied, the tone of his voice suggesting that fighting was something done only by the savages of far-off Borneo, and that he found it practically impossible to believe that his own son was involved in something so exotic and barbarian.

"Yes, sir," I said.

"With who?"

"Some other guys on the team," I replied somewhat lamely.

"They have names?"

"I don't know them," I said.

"Any of them hurt worse than you?"

"I think I loosened a couple of teeth," I said.

"It figures," he said. "One of the reasons I took this job was to give you a nice background. You're not here a week and you get in a brawl which gets you thrown off your football team."

"I'm sorry it happened," I said.

"Sorry doesn't straighten things out," my father said. "And fighting never solves anything. I thought that maybe you would have learned that somewhere along the way."

The phone rang, the extension phone on the table by his chair. He looked at it with distaste and then picked it up.

"Corelli," he said. "Yes, ma'am. Just one moment, please." He covered the microphone with his hand. "Go take a bath and put on a shirt and tie," he said. "And ask Rose to have a look at your hand."

"A shirt and tie? Who's coming to dinner?"

"A lady," he said. "I want her to get the wrong idea about us." He jerked his thumb for me to leave.

I didn't need a bath, of course, since I'd taken a shower at the stadium, so I lay on the bed when I got to my room and thought about what had happened. I hadn't been on the bed five minutes when there was a rap at the door and my brother Paul came in.

Paul must have picked up the Scotch genes. He's slight, and his skin is paler than ours and his hair is almost blond. He looked like any other nice, young, American Anglo-Saxon type except that most nice, young Anglo-Saxon types don't go around with a .357 Magnum Highway Patrolman in a shoulder holster under their sports coat.

"Well, if it isn't Battling Al, the two-fisted terror of Stockton High," he said. "Let me see the hand."

"It's all right," I said. "I had it cleaned and bandaged at school, and then Mrs. Stevens bandaged it again."

"Don't argue with me, Allan," he said. "I've had a bad day. Just let me see the hand." He sat down on the bed and jerked the bandage off. "What did you do, hit him in the mouth?"

"Yeah," I said.

"That's the worst kind of a wound, you know," he said.

"So I've been told."

"Come on in the john, and I'll put some antiseptic on it."

"I've already had antiseptic put on it."

"Be a good boy, Allan," he said, pulling me off the bed and leading me into the bathroom shared by our two rooms. "Do what you're told."

While he was fooling with the hand, I asked, "Who's the lady coming to dinner?"

"Larry's lady friend," Paul said. "Accent on lady."

"Where'd he find her?"

"You don't find ladies, dummy," Paul said. "You meet them."

"Where did he meet her?"

"I thought you'd never ask," Paul said, with a delighted smile. "In jail."

"In *jail?*"

"She's with one of those do-gooder organizations," Paul said. "They visit the prisoners. The judge assigned Larry to show her around. It was love at first sight between the bars."

Aunt Rose appeared at the bathroom door.

"Let me see your hand," she said.

"I already fixed it," Paul said.

"Your father asked me to look at the hand," Aunt Rose said. "I'm going to look at the hand."

CHAPTER 3

We usually ate about half past six, just as soon as the television news was over, but that was a special night. Larry and his lady friend weren't even due until seven.

When the news was over, my father looked at Paul. "Put on a tie," he said, "and we'll have a drink while we're waiting."

"Why do I have to wear a tie?" Paul asked.

"And change out of that ratty coat while you're at it," my father said. "I'll make you a drink while you're gone."

"So far as you know, Dad," Paul said, "Larry's lady friend may be a total teatotaler."

"She's not," my father said. "When I met her, she had an old-fashioned with her lunch."

"I think I might have a glass of wine," Aunt Rose said. I hadn't seen her. She was standing by the door to the dining room, all dressed up. This obviously was to be a big occasion.

"What's for supper?" I asked.

"Chicken cacciatore," she said.

"In that case, I'll have a little glass of wine, too," I said.

"Just don't embarrass your brother," Aunt Rose said. "This girl is obviously very important to Larry."

"Speaking of embarrassing your brother," my father said. "I don't think we should say anything about the trouble you got in. Not when this lady is here."

"Okay," I said.

"But before she gets here," my father said, "you didn't tell me the whole story."

"What do you mean?"

"About how the other guys ganged up on your friend," my father said.

"How did you find out about that?"

"That was Mrs. Stevens on the telephone before," my father said. "She called to tell me what had happened, and to apologize for giving you a beer."

"She didn't give me the beer, Keith did," I said.

"It's her house, her son, and she felt responsible," my father said.

"She's a very fine person, poor thing," Aunt Rose said.

"She asked me if you minded if I drank, and I told her no," I said.

"I told her it was all right," my father said, "but that I appreciated her calling me up. Particularly to tell me what the fight was all about."

"What was it all about?" Aunt Rose said.

"It's all right, Rose," my father said. "It's over and done with. Unless Allan, you want me to go talk to the principal?"

"No, thanks," I said. "I think the best thing to do is just let it die."

"So do I," my father said. "No matter what happened, there would always be resentment."

"But if Allan didn't do anything wrong," Aunt Rose protested.

"He knocked two teeth out, that's wrong."

"I did?"

"You loosened them pretty badly," my father said. "They may fall out." I wondered how he had learned as much as he apparently knew.

"Allan!" Aunt Rose said.

"Rose," my father said, "the only thing to do about it is nothing. Except maybe to learn to think twice the next time."

"Allan never got in trouble with anybody at Bartram," Aunt Rose said. "You'd think that here at Stockton—"

"Among the upper class, Rose?" my father asked, needling her.

"I didn't mean that," she said.

"Yes, you did," he said. "Admit it."

"All right," she said. "Okay. I'm surprised and disappointed that a fine boy like Keith Stevens and Allan should get in a fight."

"How do you know that Keith is a fine boy?" my father asked.

"From his mother. She's a fine woman. Children reflect their background."

My father laughed at her, not nastily, but because he was genuinely amused at what she said. But it made her mad anyway, and she picked up her wine glass and went into the kitchen.

"There's something you haven't thought of, Dad," Paul said, coming back wearing a necktie and another, newer sportcoat.

"What's that?"

"Larry's lady friend is liable to take one look at me and go wild," Paul said. "I mean, after all, I'm younger, better looking, and smarter than Larry."

"She probably wants a man, not a boy," my father said. "And I expect you to behave tonight. No clever remarks."

"Why not?"

"Larry's getting a little long in the tooth," my father said. "I was beginning to think he was going to hang around here forever. Let's not ruin anything."

"If you're trying to marry us off, how come you bought this big house?"

"As soon as the last of you is gone, I'm going to find a blond for myself," my father said.

"That's going to go over big with Aunt Rose," Paul said.

The doorbell rang.

"I wonder who that is?" my father asked.

"Three will get you five it's Lover Boy," Paul said.

"That's the last funny remark," my father said. "And don't bring up Battling Allan, either." He went to the door.

"Well," he said. "Welcome to our house, Barbara."

"Hello, Mr. Corelli," she said. "Thank you for having me." Paul and I looked expectantly toward the foyer for our first look at Larry's lady friend.

Paul chuckled. My father was ceremoniously shaking hands with Larry. I was tempted to giggle, but suppressed it. Paul was unable to let it go. He walked over to Larry, who was dressed in a suit, and obviously fresh from the barbershop, and grabbed his hand, enthusiastically shaking it.

"Larry," he said. "How good to see you!"

That did it, I laughed out loud.

"Barbara," he said, "these two grinning hyenas are my brothers, Paul and Allan."

"Hello," Barbara said. The word that came to my mind was "class." She was a blond, a good-looking blond, not flashy, just good looking. A lot like Keith's mother I realized.

Barbara shook Paul's hand, then mine.

"You don't look to be in very bad shape," she said, and then, "Oh, I suppose that was the wrong thing to say, wasn't it?"

"You should see the other guy," Paul said helpfully. My father glowered at him.

"And this is my Aunt Rose," Larry said, putting his arm around Aunt Rose as she came into the room. Aunt Rose was all flustered.

"I'm glad to meet you," she said.

"And I'm glad to meet you," Barbara said.

"Well," my father said. "Can I offer you a little drink, Barbara?"

"Thank you," she said.

"And then we're going to have chicken cacciatore," Aunt Rose said. "I hope you like Italian cooking?"

"Love it," Barbara said.

"What would you like?" my father asked.

"Could I have a glass of wine?" Barbara asked.

"I think I'll have a snort," Larry said.

"Snort is the noise pigs make," my father said.

"I think Larry's a little nervous, Dad," Paul said. "Doesn't he look a little nervous to you, Allan?"

"He sure does," I said.

"All right, you two," my father said. "That's enough."

"What's a nice girl like you doing with an ugly cop like him?" Paul went on.

"She's going to marry me, that's what she's going to do," Larry burst out.

"Oh, my goodness!" Aunt Rose said.

"We hadn't planned to tell you quite like this," Barbara said, blushing.

"No, we hadn't," Larry agreed. "We had—"

"If you're asking my permission," Paul said. "Forget it! Larry, you're nothing but a boy. You know nothing of the world! How can you think of marriage when I still have to tie your shoes?"

Larry stood there, torn between laughing and rage, his mouth open.

"Close your mouth, Larry," Paul said, "before you swallow a fly."

That did it. We all started to laugh, Barbara first, a nice, honest laugh. My father held his arms out to Barbara and she went to him, and he hugged her and kissed her on the forehead. Larry wrapped his arms around Paul and lifted him off the ground. Aunt Rose actually sniffled into her handkerchief, and then she rushed out of the room into the kitchen. When she came back, she had a bottle of Lambrusco, which is sort of Italian champagne, I mean it bubbles a little, not like real champagne, but a little, and a tray of good glasses. The wine was chilled, so it wasn't hard to figure out that she had known something like this was going to happen and had put it in the refrigerator ahead of time.

My father opened it, and poured it out, and raised his glass.

"To Larry and Barbara," he said, and we drank to them.

Larry and Barbara sat down on the couch, holding hands, and looking rather silly, I thought, like they were fourteen.

"Is it true you met him in jail?" Paul asked.

"In the warden's office," Barbara said. "I think you'd better remember to say that."

"Love at first sight in the slammer," Paul said. "How touching!"

"I expected some red-faced old sergeant with a whiskey voice," Barbara said.

"And I expected some skinny old maid," Larry said.

"We thought, since he arranged for us to meet, that we would get Judge Klaus to marry us," Barbara said.

"You think he did it on purpose?" Paul said.

"Possibly," my father said. "He might have figured that Barbara was what Larry needed. To get him away from his unsavory companions."

"Tell me about those, Mr. Corelli," Barbara said.

"Only after you're married," my father said. "We wouldn't want you to change your mind."

"Thanks a lot, Pop," Larry said.

"When do you plan to get married?" Aunt Rose asked.

"In a few weeks," Larry said.

"It's not like we were a couple of kids," Barbara said.

"And that way we could have some weeks off, go somewhere together, before I start my new job."

"What new job?" I asked.

"I passed the lieutenant's examination," Larry said.

"Thanks for telling me," my father said.

"I figured you'd know," Larry said.

"I did, but it would have been nice to hear it from you," my father said.

"He's a little nervous these days, Pop," Paul said. "That's why he's wearing one blue sock and one red one."

Larry looked. Paul was always able to get him that way. Barbara giggled at him.

"So what's that mean?" I asked.

"There's a vacancy on the district attorney's squad," Larry said. "He asked for me."

"Just in time, too," Paul said.

"Now, what's that supposed to mean?" Larry asked.

"You're about to burst out of your harness blues," Paul said, "particularly where you sit."

"Plainclothes job, Larry?" I asked.

"Yeah," Larry said. "It's a good job. I get paid by the county, but my seniority keeps building with the city."

"And the hours aren't bad, either," my father said. "Congratulations, Larry."

"As if you didn't know anything about it," Larry said.

"What do you mean, Larry?" Barbara asked.

"Pop and the DA go back a long way together," Larry said. "They were rookies together."

"Not that far. I was working vice when he was one of our peach-fuzz-cheeked young rookies, like Paul was."

"And you didn't say anything to him about me?"

"I didn't have to," my father said. "He's known you since you wore short pants."

"Is there any more grape, Rose?" Paul asked.

"As a matter of fact there is," Rose said, and went after it.

"I want to know something," Barbara said. "And I'd like an honest answer."

"He snores," Paul said. "You might as well face that, up front."

"What I mean is, that no one sounds as surprised as I thought you'd be," she said.

"The surprise came when he announced he was bringing you here," my father said. "That's the first time he's done that."

"I'm flattered," Barbara said.

"I was surprised," I said.

"I'm glad," she said. "Next question: Are you pleased?"

"Delighted," my father said. "Except for one thing."

"What's that?" Larry and Barbara asked, almost in duet.

"You said something about getting married in a couple of weeks," my father said. "That hardly gives us time to get things organized."

"What things?" Larry asked.

"Well, there has to be a party to announce the engagement,"

my father said. "And we can hardly have that on Wednesday and the wedding on Friday. That would leave only Thursday for the bachelor party."

"We'd sort of planned to skip all that, Pop," Larry said uncomfortably.

"Why?" my father asked, in the deceptively innocent tone of voice he sometimes used.

"Mr. Corelli," Barbara said, sounding a little embarrassed, "I don't have a family."

"You do now," my father said. "We come with him. Didn't he explain that?"

"What are you saying, Pop?" Larry asked.

"Just that it's getting a little tight if you want to get married in about three weeks. But we can handle it, don't worry. We'll announce your engagement Friday night, and you can get married two weeks later. That's not even three weeks."

"We hadn't planned on a large wedding, Mr. Corelli," Barbara said.

"Just family and a few close friends," my father said. "Just family and a few close friends."

"Oh," Barbara said.

"Watch out for him, Barbara," Paul said. "He's the Scotch-Italian Will Rogers."

"What?"

"Shut up, Paul," my father said. "I'm sure Barbara wouldn't want to deny Rose her only chance to marry off a girl, would you, Barbara?"

Barbara looked at Aunt Rose, who was beaming.

Then she started to sniffle.

"I don't know what to say."

"It's not too late to change your mind," Paul said.

"Oh," Barbara said, "I wouldn't want to do that."

"Okay, then," Pop said, "it's settled. Battling Al here, under Rose's direction, will handle everything."

"Battling Al?" Barbara asked.

"Don't ask, Barbara," Paul said. "Just take it from me that Al has nothing else to do with his spare time for the next couple of weeks."

Keith came, as he had said he would, to pick me up for school the next morning. We were still at the table. My father had just handed me a list of things to do after school, ranging from an enormous list of groceries to be picked up to a number of errands to be run in Springview and Newark.

"I'm sorry I'm early," Keith said, as I followed him out of the house.

"I was late," I said, and explained what had happened the night before. Since I was persona non grata with the Richard Stockton High School Athletic Department and had nothing better to do, I told him how I would spend the time between now and Friday. That was a Wednesday. A good deal had to be done before all our friends would gather and pretend to be surprised when Pop announced that Larry was going to marry the strange new girl no one had ever seen before.

I don't really remember what happened in school that day, except that I recall we were small-time celebrities for a brief time. The word about what had happened at the stadium had spread quickly. The guys on the team, and the guys and girls who hung around the team, pretended they couldn't see us. But there were those, too, who made it pretty clear that so far as they were concerned, the only thing we'd done wrong was not to punch out the rest of the team. I guess that was the first time I had ever really understood that not everybody in high school thinks that the institution exists just to give the jocks someplace to play ball.

Anyway when school was finally over and I started to walk home, I wasn't really at all surprised to hear the peculiar sound of the horn on Keith's Mercedes blowing at me.

I got in beside him on those fancy red-leather seats.

"Well, how does it feel to be a social reject?" Keith asked.

"If I didn't have to buy three tons of groceries for the party, I might jump off a bridge or something," I said, "out of unbearable shame."

We pulled out of the parking lot but headed in the other direction from my house.

"Hey, I'm not fooling about that stuff I have to do," I said.

"We're going to go swap cars, stupid," Keith said. "There's no way you can get all those groceries plus the folding chairs in that Ford two-door."

"You're going to help?"

"It's either that," Keith said, "or stand in the corner, wallowing in remorse about my sinful ways." At the moment Keith's eye fell on four of the jocks, headed across the street to the stadium. As he saw them, they saw him, or at least the Mercedes, which even at Stockton was an unusual car for a student to be driving. When they recognized him (or maybe the both of us) they smirked. Keith gave them the horn.

I confess, I thought it was funny. Short of chasing us down the street on foot, there was nothing they could do about it.

We drove to Keith's house. His mother wasn't home, just a maid or maybe a housekeeper, a middle-aged woman working in the kitchen, whom Keith greeted fondly and who insisted on making us something to eat. We shared a triple-decker club sandwich, as good as any I've ever had in a restaurant. And we had a beer. Or I had one and Keith had two. I would have rather had a glass of milk, but I wasn't given a choice. The beer was sitting on the kitchen table when I sat down. Keith had put it there.

Afterward we got in the Ford station wagon and hit the Acme Supermarket. Then we drove into Newark and picked up two dozen folding chairs at my father's VFW post, and then finally back to Springview.

My father's car was there, and we had barely opened the doors when he came charging out of the house. I could tell by the sheepish look on his face what had happened. When I hadn't come home to pick up the Ford, Rose had gotten excited and called him.

"You should have called Rose," he said.

"I guess that's my fault, Mr. Corelli," Keith said. "I—"

"It's his fault," my father said, cutting him off. "You get everything?"

"Yes, sir."

"Next time make sure Rose knows what you're up to," he said.

"Yes, sir."

"He drafted you, did he?" Pop asked, turning to Keith.

"I guess it would be more accurate to say I enlisted," Keith said. "I just couldn't find it in my manly heart to see this fragile child trying to carry all those heavy chairs himself."

My father laughed.

"You're a pair of delicate flowers all right," he said. "I'll give you a hand with the stuff."

CHAPTER 4

We had barely finished carrying the chairs and the groceries into the house when the doorbell (it was a chime actually) went off. I pulled the door open and found myself looking at a very short, very muscular man wearing coveralls and carrying two strange leather objects in his hands.

"I got your carpet, Charley," he said. "You ready for me?"

"Huh?"

"I'm from Danziger's," he said, as if that explained everything. Parked behind Keith's station wagon was a large truck with "Danziger's" written in large gold script on the side.

I looked at him again.

"I'm the layer," he said.

"Pop!" I called, and my father came to the door.

"You're late," he said to the muscular little man.

"You ready for me?" the little man replied.

"Not quite," my father said. "The muscle just got home."

"You and him going to do it?" the little man asked. "I'm a layer. I don't move furniture."

"So Mr. Danziger told me," my father said. "Come on in and show me what you want done."

Keith had shown up by then, out of curiosity, and the little man pushed him out of the way with one of the leather things he had in his hands. He followed my father into the living room. He sat down on the couch and strapped the leather things over his knees. Then he took a curved knife from a sheath on his belt, dropped to his knees, and moved with surprising speed across the floor to the opening between the living room and the dining room. He bent over and examined the carpet very closely.

"It's shot," he announced. It was a professional decision.

"That's why I'm replacing it," my father said.

"I mean, there's nothing here worth salvaging," the little man said. "If you had that in mind."

"I didn't," my father said.

"Okay," the little man said. He pointed at Keith and me with his knife. "You guys move everything in here," he said, pointing to the living room, "in there." He indicated the dining room. "But to do that, you're going to have to make room, you understand?"

"Yes, sir," Keith said, smiling.

"So start," the little man said. Then he took his knife and stabbed it in the carpet, lifting it four or five inches off the floor. He examined it carefully, let it drop to the floor, and stabbed it again, a few inches away from the first place.

"There it is," he said, with satisfaction in his voice. He let the carpet drop again, and then made a cutting slash with the knife. He put his fingers in the carpet, lifted, and then ran the knife quickly and smoothly in a line. The carpet split. He looked up at us.

"The seam," he said. "You didn't really think it came in one piece, did you?"

"To tell you the truth," Keith said, "I never gave it much thought."

"You want to start moving the furniture now?" the little man asked.

Keith and I went into the dining room, picked up the table, and moved it into a corner. Then we moved the chairs, so there would be room for the living-room furniture. My father leaned on the wall and watched. It wasn't, I thought, that he was lazy. It was just that he was used to supervising other people.

As we moved the furniture, the little man worked his way around the room on his knees, cutting the carpet about six inches from the wall. By the time we had all the furniture out, he had rolled the carpet up.

Now he scurried around the room on his leather kneepads, examining the pad underneath from a distance of about four inches, and from time to time banging it with his fist. There was something comical about the whole thing, but it wasn't the sort of thing that made you want to laugh out loud. He was obviously not only dead serious about what he was doing, but expert as well.

"The pad's all right," he announced finally. "That'll save you some money, Chief. I tell people, you buy the best pad, you'll save money in the long run, but they don't listen." He turned to us again. "Okay," he said, "pick up the carpet and get it outside."

The roll of carpet was heavier than it looked, and when we

finally managed to lift the ends off the floor, it started to buckle in the middle.

"You better grab the middle, Chief," the little man said. I bit my lip to keep from laughing or smiling, because it wasn't often that I heard someone order my father around. But without a word my father walked to the center of the rolled-up carpet and put his arm around it. The three of us, staggering, got it outside the house.

"Dump it on the lawn for now," the little man said. "You can load it in the truck later." When we had done that, he pointed to one of maybe half a dozen paper-wrapped rolls in the truck. "Bring that one in first," he said. "But only when I tell you." And with that he walked back in the house.

The three of us smiled at each other, and then followed him back in. He was on his knees again, working on the strip of carpet remaining against the walls. He had a new gadget, this one a sort of flat fork, about six inches wide. The handle of it was a large leather ball. He stuck the end with the points into the carpet, hit the leather end with the heel of his hand, and loosened the carpet from what had held it right against the walls, an inch-wide strip of wood with needles mounted in it, pointing away from the room.

"Until just now," Keith said. "I thought they just nailed it in place."

"Me, too," my father said, chuckling. And then he had another thought.

"You don't have to do this, Keith," he said.

"Wouldn't miss it for the world," Keith said. "I want to see if he can put it down as quick as he takes it up."

"Won't your mother be wondering about you?" my father asked.

"I'll call her and tell her where I am," Keith said. He spotted the telephone cord and followed it into the dining room, where he found the telephone on one of the armchairs we had moved.

By this time the carpet layer had all the carpet loosened from one wall. He sliced it neatly with his hook-bladed knife, and then gestured at me.

"Roll that up," he ordered, "and get it out of here."

I did what I was told to do, and when I came in from outside, I was sort of surprised to see my father talking on the phone.

"What I thought I would do, Mrs. Stevens," he said, "since it's too confused around here to think about cooking, is to take my sister Rose and the boys out to the Villa Scarlatti for supper. Would it be all right with you?"

I couldn't hear what she said in reply, but then he went on.

"In that case why don't you come along with us? Do you like Italian food?"

Keith looked at me. Our eyebrows rose.

"Well the way this fellow's working," my father said, "it won't take long. What about seven?" Pause. "Fine. Look forward to seeing you again. Good-bye, Mrs. Stevens."

"Okay, Muscles," the little man said to Keith. "Get this out of here."

My father turned to me. "We're going to pick up Mrs. Stevens on our way to supper," he said. "I met her when I gave a talk to the League of Women Voters."

"Go out and give the other guy a hand with the carpet," the little man ordered. My father and I dutifully marched out of the living room and, with Keith, pulled and tugged the first of four rolls of carpet out of the Danziger's truck. It seemed a lot heavier than the old carpet we'd carried out.

The muscular little man waited for us inside. He ripped the heavy, brown, Kraft paper cover of the carpet with his hooked knife, snatched it completely off with one quick, graceful gesture, and then directed us, with tiny movement of his hands, how to line it up against the front wall. We were all having a hard time keeping from smiling at his precision, for it looked at first that it didn't really matter how the roll was placed.

But he knew, of course, what he was doing. He unrolled just enough of the carpet to give him room to get on his knees between the roll and the fastening strip against the wall. Then he took the forklike tool in his hands and with a series of raps against its leather handle, moving all the time on his knees, quickly had that end of the carpet locked in place. Then he turned around, dropped the tool, and spreading his arms as wide as they would go, started to unroll the carpet. The side against the wall fit perfectly. As he scuttled along on his knees, I realized why he had made us place the roll with such precision. All he was going to have to do now was go down the far side and trim the carpet to size with his hooked knife. He wasn't going to have to shift the carpet around on the floor at all.

We watched as he fastened one side to the wall and then scuttled across the floor to work on the other side. When he was about halfway down the side which opened onto the foyer, and without bothering to turn around and look at us, he gave the next order: "Okay," he said. "Start moving the stuff in the dining room in here."

He was finished staking the living room carpet in place long before we had moved the living-room furniture back in place. He leaned on the wall and watched us work. By the time we had the dining-room furniture moved into the living room, he had cut the dining-room carpet and started to roll it up. He followed us outside and showed us which roll of new carpet to bring in.

After we had shifted the second roll of carpet in place, he gave us permission to load the old carpet on the truck. Twenty minutes later the muscular little man was surveying, with a critical eye, his finished work.

"Not bad," he said. "There's a couple of uneven spots, but they'll settle all right."

I couldn't see any uneven places. It looked perfect to me.

"How about a glass of wine?" my father asked.

"Just one," the little man said. "I've got one more job today."

Keith and I moved the dining room furniture back in place as my father got the wine. Then we collapsed on the couch.

"Do you always work so fast?" my father asked.

"I don't work for Danziger's," the little man said. "I work on contract for so much a square yard. The faster it goes down, the more money I make." He tossed down the glass of red wine and handed the empty glass to my father. "You have any problems with it, Chief," he said, "you let me know."

He nodded at Keith and me, shook my father's hand, and left.

For some reason, although all we'd contributed was muscle, we had a fine feeling of satisfaction. With a wide smile on his face my father crossed to where Keith and I were sitting and handed us each a glass. Then he handed Keith the bottle and sat down in his armchair.

"I really expected Danziger's to have the place torn up all day," he said, "and tomorrow."

"Tomorrow," Keith said, "he's going to recarpet the State Capitol Building."

"In the morning," I said. We all laughed.

Aunt Rose came in from the kitchen.

"I can't believe it," she said, examining the carpet. My Aunt Rose is my father's oldest sister. She's about twenty years older than he is. About the time that my mother died, her husband passed on, and with her children grown she just moved in with us and started to raise another family.

"If he can put a whole new carpet down in about two hours," my father said, "how come it takes you all morning to vacuum it?"

"Just don't spill any of that wine on it," Aunt Rose said. "It's beautiful."

"Danziger's said it was wine-proof," my father said. "I told them we spill a lot of wine, and that was important."

"I'll bet you did," she said. "Why don't we send Al out for some fried chicken? I'm in no mood to cook."

"We're all going out for dinner," my father said. "Keith and his mother, too."

"Al's not going like that," Rose said, indicating my school clothes.

"I'll have to change, too," Keith said. He sniffed. "And shower, too. I'm not used to manual labor. I generally work with my brain."

My father chuckled.

"Why don't I just go home and change and get Mother?" he said.

"Good idea," my father said, "but finish your wine."

"Good idea," Keith parroted, and filled his glass from the bottle. Then he stood up and drank it down. "I won't be long," he said, as he walked out.

"A little water wouldn't melt you, either," Aunt Rose said to me. I started upstairs. I overheard Rose speaking softly to my father.

"That's a nice boy, Paul," she said. "I'm happy for Al."

"Maybe their getting kicked off the football team was a good thing after all."

"I think so too, but don't let him know," Aunt Rose said.

When I came back downstairs, Aunt Rose had changed her dress and immediately put me to work straightening the furniture. A couple of minutes later, my father, fresh from his shower, came into the room. He helped himself to a glass of wine, gave one to Rose, and settled in his chair. And a few minutes after that we heard the squeal of tires on the driveway.

I let Keith and his mother in, and I remember thinking again that she looked more like somebody's girl friend than somebody's mother.

"Welcome to our home, Mrs. Stevens," my father said, standing behind me.

"I hope I'm not intruding, Chief Corelli," she said. She gave me a little smile.

"And this is my sister, Mrs. Portman," my father said. "But you've met, haven't you?"

"It's nice to see you again," Aunt Rose said.

"Enough of this social small talk," Keith said. "Come see the fruit of my labor, Mother."

The telephone rang.

"Rose, offer Mrs. Stevens a glass of wine," my father said. "I've been expecting that call."

I noticed that as my father headed for the telephone in the den, where he took his telephone calls, that Keith's mother's eyes dropped to the butt of the Chief's Special sticking out of his belt. I had learned that guns sometimes affect people strangely; she was apparently no different. It was also obvious to me that Aunt Rose and Keith's mother had made a snap judgment: they liked each other. That wasn't surprising, when I thought about it. They were the same kind of women, the only difference being that Aunt Rose was older. I suddenly realized they were both widows. And Aunt Rose's husband, whom I barely remembered, had been a lawyer. Lawyers are a lot more like stockbrokers than policemen.

My father was shrugging into his suit jacket when he came back in the room.

"Crime, for the moment," he said, "organized and amateur, seems to be under control. Shall we go get something to eat?"

Mrs. Stevens had brought the Mercedes sedan. It blocked the other cars in the driveway, and it was the obvious car to take. She asked my father if he would mind driving. I wondered if she were just being polite, or whether she had somehow learned that my father firmly believed he was the only competent driver on the highway. Anyway Keith and I got in the back with Aunt Rose, and my father and Mrs. Stevens were up front.

Just before we reached the border between South Orange and Springview, I heard the whoop-whoop-whoop of a police car, and when I turned and looked out the window, there was a Springview Police Department Chevrolet, gumball machine flashing, gaining on us. My father pulled to the right and slowed down. The police car drew parallel, and then cut in front of us. My father braked sharply.

"Uh oh," he said. "I guess I spoke too quickly about crime being under control."

The cop in the police car bounced out of the car and strode importantly back to us.

"How do I get this window to go down?" my father asked. Mrs. Stevens leaned over in front of him and worked the switch that lowered the window. The cop put both his hands on the window and lowered his face to look at the driver. His look of righteous indignation, which had sort of confused me, vanished. It was replaced by a look of red-faced embarrassment.

"Good evening, Chief," he said. "Anything I can do for you?"

Keith started to giggle. So did I. Aunt Rose gave me a sharp elbow in the ribs.

"Not that I can think of," my father said coldly. "I haven't had a chance to learn everybody's name yet. What's yours?"

"Lawton, Chief," the cop said.

"Anything else on your mind?" my father asked.

"No, sir," the cop said.

My father ran the window up and pulled back onto the road.

There was sort of a hush in the car. Aunt Rose and I knew, of course, that my father was furious. When that icy tone enters his voice, the thing to do is say absolutely nothing. Mrs. Stevens couldn't have known this, of course, but she wasn't the kind to make flip remarks. Keith was.

"Anything I can do for you, Chief?" he asked, "any little thing at all?"

My father turned around and glowered at Keith. For a moment I thought he was going to blow up, which would, of course, ruin the evening. But then he laughed.

"I guess I did ruin his evening," he said. "I hope I did."

"What was that all about, Mr. Corelli?" Keith's mother asked. There was laughter in her voice now, too. The look on the cop's face when he saw Pop was really funny.

"Well, I suspect my major violation of the law was to drive this fancy automobile," my father said. "And that's not really funny. I'll have someone give that young fella a little talk."

"I don't quite understand," Mrs. Stevens said.

"Well, one of the reasons this job came open was because there was a lot of talk going around that law enforcement wasn't exactly level-handed," my father said. "So when I took over, I spread the word around that the fix was off."

"What's that got to do with him stopping us?" Mrs. Stevens asked.

"I'm not sure," my father said. "But I have the feeling that he was going to hand me a ticket not because I was a couple of miles over the limit, but because I was driving a Mercedes. Giving out bad tickets is just as bad as having tickets fixed."

"Were you speeding?" Mrs. Stevens asked.

"No, I was driving safely," my father said. "And I put that word out too, that what we're supposed to do is keep the highways safe, not keep a record of how many traffic citations are issued."

"Do they do that?"

"They used to," my father said. "A patrolman was sometimes judged on how many tickets he passed out. That's lousy police work."

"I really don't know anything about it," Mrs. Stevens said. "You're the first policeman I've ever really known."

"I didn't mean to bore you with all this," my father said.

"Not at all," Mrs. Stevens said. "I'm fascinated. All I know about the police is what we see on television."

"You don't see what it's like on television," my father said flatly. "They couldn't show you the real stuff on TV, and the rest of it is mostly boring."

By then we were across the city border and into South Orange, and I could see the red neon sign of the Villa Scarlatti up ahead.

We'd been coming to the Villa Scarlatti all my life. I don't know whether my father was always a friend of Mr. Scarlatti (for that matter of the whole Scarlatti family) and that was why we had gone there so often, or whether they had become friends because we had gone there so much. But in any event they knew us pretty well, and there was interest in Mr. Scarlatti's eyes when he saw Mrs. Stevens.

He came out of his office just as soon as we walked in the door, and he led us around the line of people waiting for tables.

"Jerry, these are our friends, the Stevens," my father began, after we sat down.

"Oh, I know Mrs. Stevens," Jerry Scarlatti said. "Nice to see you again."

"Hello, Jerry," Mrs. Stevens said.

He looked at us. "I hate to see how big these two have grown," he said, beaming at Keith and me. "They make me realize how old we're all getting."

That sort of remark used to bother me. But about a year ago it had occurred to me that when someone said I was "big," it wasn't a relative term. I was taller then, and about as heavy as my father, and Keith had a couple of inches and maybe twenty pounds on me. I was not only big, I was bigger, and Keith was even bigger than me.

A waiter brought a bottle of Lambrusco and a handful of glasses held by their stems.

"Compliments of the house, Paul," Mr. Scarlatti said.

"The only reason he does that," my father said to Mrs. Stevens, "is to shame you into ordering something expensive."

"Evil to him who evil thinks," Scarlatti said, opening the bottle and pouring wine in all the glasses. I suppose that was technically illegal, as neither Keith nor I was eighteen, but it wasn't the same thing as if we had walked in alone into the bar of Villa Scarlatti and ordered a couple of martinis on the rocks. For one thing there was an Italian flavor to it. The Corellis and the Scarlattis were Italian, or mostly Italian, and a glass of wine with a meal is not considered "drinking." For another my father and aunt and Keith's mother were there. And finally, I suppose, it was highly unlikely that some South Orange cop would march in the place and haul the Springview Chief of Police off to the slammer for serving minors alcohol.

"To good food and good friends," my father said, raising his glass. Mr. Scarlatti, as well as everybody else, raised his glass.

"I've got some very nice veal," Mr. Scarlatti said, "with mushrooms and green peppers, sautéed in butter with a little garlic?"

"Sounds delicious," Mrs. Stevens said.

"All around?" my father asked, looking at us one at a time.

CHAPTER 5

I could never remember my father talking so much. He said things to Mrs. Stevens that he had never said to us. Or he told her things which explained what I'd heard him, all my life, tell my brothers or talk about with other cops.

I'd heard him say, a thousand times I suppose, that cops are supposed to be part of the community, not sitting on top of it, and that the cop's first responsibility is to get the community to understand what he's doing and why. But that night for the first time, I got to understand his reasoning.

"I was in the Army during the Korean War, Mrs. Stevens—" he began, and she interrupted him.

"Why don't you call me Virginia?" she asked.

"All right," he said, and I thought he blushed a little. "Virginia. My first name is Paul."

"You were saying you were in the Korean War?"

"No. I was in the Army *during* the Korean War," my father corrected. "They sent me to Europe. I was a Military Police Captain assigned to the Communications Zone in France, which meant I was stationed in Paris."

"Very nice," Mrs. Stevens said.

"We worked with the French police," he said, "and that really opened my eyes to what a good system we have here."

"You mean the French police aren't very good?" she asked.

"Depends on what you mean by good," he said. "Sure, they're good. But their whole philosophy is different, and their relationship with the people is different."

"I don't think I understand," she said.

"Well," he said, "I don't really know how to explain, but let me try to put it this way. Supposing I hadn't been driving tonight and that cop had given you a ticket. What would you have done about it?"

"You mean if I hadn't been speeding?"

"Yes."

"I'd have gone to see the chief of police first thing in the morning," Mrs. Stevens said. "And told him what I thought about it."

"That's what I mean," my father said. "If you don't like the way the cops treat you, you can complain. Now as a practical matter, not knowing you personally I mean, if you had come to see me I probably would have supported the cop. But I would have kept an eye on him. Talked to his captain about the complaint. And if we got more than one complaint, say two or three people complaining that they had been ticketed unfairly, that cop would have a sergeant practically living with him to make sure that he wasn't abusing his power."

"And that doesn't happen in France?"

"The French police, the Gendarmerie, answer to nobody but themselves. They think of themselves as being apart from the rest of society. You would get nowhere going to a police station and saying you felt you were unjustly ticketed."

"Why is that?"

"It goes back a long way," my father said. "I really looked into it. It goes back to the beginning of police forces. In Europe the first cops worked for the king or the duke—the man in the castle. He picked three men and told them to keep the people in the village in line. If you didn't like the way they did it, you complained to the king. People don't complain to kings very often."

"It was different here?"

"Absolutely," my father said. "The first cops in America, after the Revolution of course, were guys picked and hired by the people to keep order. Maybe only part time. Say a bunch of farmers got together every Friday night at a tavern and started getting a little out of hand late at night. The city council, or whatever the local government was, hired one of the farmers to keep order. If he couldn't handle it well, the farmers would complain, and they'd fire him and get somebody who could do the job."

"What about the police in New York and other big cities?" Mrs. Stevens asked. She was obviously fascinated by Pop's little lecture. "Forgive me, Paul, but isn't it true that they were mostly Irish immigrants, and Italian, as low on the ladder as they could be? And working for the establishment?"

"That's the whole point," my father said. "As crooked as some of those politicians were, they still held office because they were voted into it. And one of the reasons they kept getting reelected was because, right or wrong, the people trusted them; and one of the reasons the people trusted them was because they not only kept the police in line, but put the Irish and Italian immigrants on the force. The policeman the people had to deal with, the cop on the beat in the Irish neighborhood, was a part of the community, an Irish immigrant himself, instead of somebody else just put in charge."

"That's an interesting thought," Mrs. Stevens said.

"The most important part of it is that the cop thought of himself as part of the community. He owed his allegiance to the neighborhood, to his people."

"And it's not that way in France? In Europe?"

"When I was in France," my father said, "I got to know some of the higher-ups in the Gendarmerie pretty well. One time I asked a fellow, an inspector, what he had done during the war when the Germans occupied France."

"And?"

"He looked at me kind of funny and said that he'd been a policeman, of course."

"You mean he'd been a collaborator? And admitted it?"

"No. He didn't think he was a collaborator, and the French people didn't think he was a collaborator, either."

"But the Germans kept him on as a policeman?"

"That's the whole point. The Germans didn't even disarm the police. One day they were working for the French government, and the next day for the Germans."

"And the French people didn't see anything wrong with this? They didn't hate the police for just going to work for the Germans?"

"They hated the police before the Germans took over. Nothing

was really changed. That really made me think about the difference. And it isn't only the French. When the American Army
moved into Germany, when the MPs moved in right after the in-
fantry, the first thing we did was disarm the police and start to
organize a new police force. The Germans couldn't understand
that. The German police would have been perfectly willing to
swap sides just as the French had done. They worked for who-
ever was in charge. They didn't work *for* the people. They *policed*
the people."

"And it wouldn't have been that way here?" she asked.

"I don't think so," my father said very seriously. "I like to think
that if the Germans ever took Newark, they'd have had to wipe
out the police force first. I think American cops believe they have
a duty to protect the people, not just police them."

"Paul," Aunt Rose said, "you sound as if you're giving a speech."
My father flushed.

"Sorry," he said. "I guess I got carried away."

"Not at all," Mrs. Stevens said. She reached out and touched
my father's hand. "I've been fascinated. I never thought about
any of this before."

"I've never heard him talk like this before," Aunt Rose said.
It really wasn't the most tactful thing she could have said. My
father glowered at her, and then Mrs. Stevens became aware that
she was touching his hand. She took hers away as if it were
burned.

"Tell me something, Chief," Keith said.

"Sure," my father said. "What?"

"Is there anything I can do for you? Any little thing at all?"

There was a moment's silence, and then we all started to laugh
loudly, even Aunt Rose. People at other tables turned to look at
us. Aunt Rose shushed us.

My father picked up the bottle of Lambrusco and tried to fill

Aunt Rose's glass. The bottle was empty. He looked around, caught the waiter's eye, and signaled for another.

The antipasto was delivered right after the wine, and Mrs. Stevens changed the subject, got the conversation going again.

"Keith tells me your son is getting married," she said. That gave Aunt Rose a chance to get into the conversation. Barbara's all-around virtues were discussed at some length along with the somewhat delicate subject of Barbara not having a family, which meant that the Corellis, as Aunt Rose put it, would have to be on both sides of the aisle during the wedding.

"The engagement's going to be announced tomorrow night," Aunt Rose said. "We'd love to have you with us, Virginia, and I'm sure Barbara would be grateful if you were there."

"Why do you say that?" Mrs. Stevens said.

"If you could come," Aunt Rose said, "that would mean there would be two of you who weren't either Corellis, or Italians, or cops, or all three."

"I'd love to come," Mrs. Stevens said. "Thank you for asking me."

"I'll drink to that," Keith said, helping himself to another glass of wine. It didn't seem to be the right kind of a remark, and I looked at him. His eyes were bright. I smiled. Keith was a little gassed. I wondered if the others could see this. If they did, no one said anything to him. What I thought at the time was that he wasn't used to the Lambrusco, that it was stronger than he thought.

I don't remember anything special about the rest of the evening, except that the veal was delicious, and that everybody laughed a lot. Keith was more than a little silly. The wine had really gotten to him. But he didn't do anything wrong, and I didn't think much about it.

I woke up the next morning to the smell of food. Not a smell of

frying bacon—breakfast food—but the smell of what we would
serve that night for dinner. When I got dressed and went downstairs, Paul and Larry and my father were sitting at the dining-
room table. That was unusual because we always ate breakfast in
the kitchen. When I went in the kitchen, the place looked like
the kitchen at Villa Scarlatti during their rush hour. My aunt Lois
and her married daughter, my cousin Frances, had either volunteered to help Aunt Rose or had been drafted. There was a turkey
in the oven, another one sitting on the sink waiting for its turn, a
boiled ham, and Frances was in the process of boning a large
fresh ham on the kitchen table.

Aunt Rose quickly fried me a couple of eggs, put them on a
plate with some already-cooked bacon and some already-cold
toast, handed the plate and a glass of milk to me, and ushered me
back out of the kitchen.

I sat down with my brothers and father.

"It's like Thanksgiving," I said.

"An occasion of great joy," Paul said. "We're finally getting rid
of Larry."

"Drop dead," Larry said.

"Does your intended fully understand what she's getting into?"
Paul asked.

"Like what?"

"Like these Roman food orgies?" Paul asked. "Can she cook,
Larry?"

"Gee," Larry said, "I really don't know."

"She probably thinks an Italian banquet is a six-pack and pizza,"
Paul said.

"Oh, shut up," Larry said. "I'm sure she can cook." He didn't
sound very sure.

"You could live on love alone for the first couple of months, I
suppose," Paul said. "But after that—"

"I'm sure she can cook," Larry said firmly.

"And if she can't," my father said, "Rose can teach her."

"How does she feel about women's lib, Larry? Did she make you sign a written agreement that you'll wash the dishes?"

"Will you knock it off?" Larry said. He got to his feet. He walked to the front hall, and then turned and called out to me, "Your limousine is here, your highness."

"Ask the chauffeur if he'd like some breakfast," I replied. "I always like to be nice to the lower classes."

Keith came in a moment or so later, politely rejected an offer of something to eat, and then helped himself to a piece of my bacon.

"I don't want you two vanishing this afternoon," my father said, "like yesterday. Rose'll have plenty for Al to do."

"Yes, sir," Keith said politely. "Mother said if I saw you I was to tell you what a nice time she had last night."

"We all had a good time last night."

"Everybody but a certain cop," Keith corrected him.

"Huh?" Paul asked. "What cop?"

"I was ambling along," my father said, "minding my own business and obeying the speed limit, and one of my eager youngsters, who's probably got a thing against Mercedes—"

"What Mercedes?"

"Virginia's," my father said, and then hastily corrected himself. "Mrs. Stevens's. She and Keith had supper with us last night."

"What about the cop?" Paul asked.

"Let's just say he was very surprised to see me at the wheel of the Mercedes," my father said.

"He probably thinks you're on the take," Paul said. "The word will be all over the force by now."

"I don't think that's funny, Paul," my father said.

"How else could a cop afford a car like that?" Paul asked.

"He could have saved his money," I said.

"Or hit the daily double at Monmouth," Paul added, joking. Monmouth is the race track in South Jersey. "What did he say?"

"He asked me if there was anything he could do for me," my father said.

"You going to jump on him?"

"I intend to have a word with his captain," my father said.

"We were all eager at first," Paul said. "You too, probably."

"I never handed out tickets for the fun of it," my father said too firmly. Then he joked, "But I do recall examining myself in the full-length mirror outside Bamberger's on Market Street and thinking what a splendid figure I cut in my uniform." We chuckled and he went on. "I'm not going to suspend him or anything like that. But he won't forget last night for a while, either."

"We gotta go," Keith said to me, and we left.

In the car, as we started down the hill toward Stockton High, Keith said, "I almost put my foot in my mouth just now."

"How?"

"There's another way a poor but honest cop can afford a car like this," he said. "And I almost said it."

"What do you mean?"

"He could marry a rich widow."

He looked at me with a "see-how-clever-and-funny-I-am" look on his face, and I dutifully laughed. But there was no smile in his eyes, and what he had said wasn't really funny.

It wasn't far to school fortunately, so there was really no need for me to think of something to say in reply. And I didn't think much about it. My first period was a study hall, and I had to use it to do the homework I hadn't done the night before.

Despite the speech my father had given us about Aunt Rose having a lot for us to do after school, the only thing we had to do was go over to Gruning's Bakery in South Orange to pick up a tray of little cakes—one thousand calories to the bite—that Aunt Rose had ordered baked specially for us.

Keith followed me in the door of the bakery. I stopped and gave him an elbow in the ribs. "Look at that!" I said. While someone of my charm, all-around good looks, and vast experience with the fair sex is generally immune to female charms, the blond standing in front of the glass display case with her mother was the exception that proved the rule. The old-fashioned word that came to my mind was a word my father used to describe a woman who was, all around, something special: stunning.

"You like that, huh?" Keith asked.

"I like that," I said.

"Well, then," he said, and pushed past me.

"Hey!" I said, to stop him. It was too late.

He walked up to the girl's mother.

"Pardon me, madam," he said. "I have a small problem."

"What's that?" the woman said, sort of smiling.

"I have this friend," Keith said. "He's not too bright, but he's strong and honest, and he was just stricken by your daughter's all-around beauty and whatever. Could you find it in your heart to permit me to introduce them?"

The woman looked over at me. I wanted to sink through the floor. The girl looked at me and then away in embarrassment.

"Have you got him on a leash?" the mother asked.

"He's well trained," Keith said. "When I say 'heel,' he sits down and licks my hand."

"In that case . . . ," the mother said.

"Al," Keith called to me. "Come over and meet my friends." There was nothing for me to do but walk over.

"This is Al Corelli," Keith said.

"What's a nice boy like you, Al," the mother asked, "doing with a bum like Keith Stevens?"

"That's not very nice," Keith said. "I'll tell Mother you've been beastly to me again."

"I just talked to your mother," the woman said. "It was the first I'd heard you hadn't gone back to school. And she told me about your friend, too." She put out her hand to me. "I'm Lois Withers," she said. "I was Mrs. Stevens's roommate in college. And I'm Ape-boy's godmother."

"How do you do?" I said somewhat lamely.

"And this is my daughter, Marilyn," Mrs. Withers said.

"Hi," I said.

"Hi," she repeated. She smiled. "He didn't tell you he knew us, right? He let you think he was just walking over to strangers and coming on strong?"

I nodded.

"I could tell by the look on your face," she said. "He's always had a weird sense of humor."

"If you're interested in that sort of thing," Keith said, "I have an interesting collection of photographs of Blondie here and me frolicking on a rug in our birthday suits. We were eight months old, or so."

"Oh, shut up, Keith," Marilyn said.

"The reason I called your mother, Keith," Mrs. Withers said, "was to see if you might be home over the weekend."

"Oh?"

"Marilyn's having her party, a birthday dance at the club, and I thought you should be there."

"Don't let it go to your head," Marilyn said. "There's a shortage of men. Everybody's away at school."

"In that case," Keith said, "I presume the invitation includes my pal? Since you're scraping the bottom of the manpower barrel?"

"Your mother," Mrs. Withers said, "did mention him."

"Unfortunately," Keith began, "the press of our extensive social obligations—" He looked at me. I must have had disappointment written all over my forehead with a grease pencil. He finished the sentence "—isn't pressing enough to think of a polite way to refuse."

"Thanks a lot," Marilyn said.

"Don't be such a louse, Keith," Mrs. Withers said. "A lot of your friends will be there."

"Impossible," he said.

"What do you mean, impossible?"

"You're looking at the only friend I've ever had," Keith said.

"A lot of that is your own fault," Mrs. Withers said, sounding, I realized, like a mother or an aunt. There was love and exasperation in her voice.

"What time does the orgy start?" Keith asked.

"Half past seven."

"We'll be there," Keith said. "And now if you will excuse me," he switched to a thick, mock-German accent, "I must go and put Benzene in der Mercedes." He looked at me. "I'll either be outside or in the Texaco station." He walked out of the bakery.

Mrs. Withers looked at me.

"Tell me something," she said. "Did I read that right?"

"I beg your pardon?"

"Did he agree to come because he thought you wanted to?"

"I guess so," I replied, after a long, embarrassing pause.

"He's a strange boy," Mrs. Withers said.

The salesclerk finally showed up.

"I'll be with you in just a moment, Mrs. Withers," she said. "Can I help you?"

"My name is Corelli," I said. "My aunt, Mrs. Portman, ordered some cakes."

"Right here," she said, taking a two-foot square, foil-covered tray from the display case.

"I'll get the door for you," Marilyn said, and walked to it in front of me. "Tell me something," she said softly.

"What?"

"Is it true that you two punched out the Stockton football team?"

"Just the backfield," I said.

"Huh," she snorted. Then she smiled. "I'll see you Saturday, Al. Thanks for making Keith come."

I started walking toward the Texaco station on the corner.

CHAPTER 6

"Let me have your attention a moment," my father said loudly, but not loudly enough to catch everybody's attention. He picked up an empty bottle of Lambrusco and hit it with the handle of a knife, so that it rang like a bell.

The noise of conversation in the room died. He was standing in the living room behind the bar. The bar was actually the television set, pulled away from the wall, covered with a layer of tinfoil in case anything got spilled and with a tablecloth hanging to the ground.

"You may all be wondering," he said, "why I asked you here tonight." There was laughter at that. "And it is not because the Civil Service Commission made a large clerical error and certified my oldest son as a lieutenant." More laughter. "An even larger error has been made," Pop went on. "An otherwise intelligent, and I must add beautiful and charming young woman, who certainly doesn't know what she's letting herself in for, has taken pity on Rose and me. She realizes what a strain it is on people our age to have to take care of someone like Larry." More laughter.

"Getting someone his size out of bed and off to work in the morning with his face washed, his nose blown, his shoes shined, and his necktie straight, and with a string tied to his finger to remind him to eat lunch is obviously something old folks shouldn't have to do. Miss Barbara Mallon has graciously volunteered to assume that responsibility.

"Family, friends, with great pride and happiness I announce the engagement of Barbara and Larry. I ask that you drink with me to their marriage and happiness."

There was applause at that, and on cue Keith and I popped the corks of bottles of champagne and quickly filled trays of glasses, which Aunt Rose and Cousin Frances passed around to the people in the room.

I thought that if Barbara hadn't known what she was getting into, she knew now. With the exception of Keith's mother, everybody in the house—fifty, sixty people—was Italian, some kind of a cop (even the District Attorney was there, both as Pop's old friend and Larry's new boss), or a relative, and most of the time either all three or at least married to somebody who was.

As soon as the toast was drunk, everybody stood in line to shake Larry's and Pop's hands, to kiss Barbara, and then to get in line in front of Keith and me again to have their glasses refilled.

The next thing I remember was an hour or so later, when things had gotten a lot more informal. That many people in the house had raised the temperature, and the men removed their jackets. Some were sitting on the floor to eat the food from the buffet.

I remember that Keith cracked, "I'm glad I know all these people are cops." I didn't understand him at first, but then I realized he wasn't used to seeing a room full of people, with two out of three of the men carrying pistols on their hips.

I remember seeing Pop, when I made a sweep through the house, picking up empty glasses and dirty plates and emptying ashtrays. He and Mr. Bigglemann, the District Attorney, were sitting on the couch with Mrs. Stevens between them, telling her stories, the three of them red-faced from laughing.

Aunt Rose, of course, kept me busy keeping the mess under control. I didn't really mind, and I was really touched when I walked past Barbara one time and she grabbed my arm and pulled me close and stood on her toes and kissed me on the cheek.

"Thanks, Allan," she said.

And about five minutes after that, as I was walking through the hall toward the kitchen, Paul grabbed me and pulled me into the little room Pop used as an office.

"Have you been drinking?" he demanded, not at all pleasantly. "Are you bombed?"

"What gave you that idea?"

He looked at me closely, shrugged, told me to put the tray of dirty plates I was carrying down on Pop's desk, and then led me outside the house. Two of his friends were standing by Keith's Mercedes. Keith was in the front-passengers' seat, slumped into it, his head against the headrest, a stupid smile on his face.

"He was in the downstairs john, tossing his cookies," Paul said with disgust.

"Ah, there you are, old buddy," Keith said. "I was wondering what happened to you."

"What happened to you?" I asked, although I already knew.

"It must have been something I ate," he said. "Nothing whatever to worry about."

"Something he ate!" one of the guys standing by the open door said. He was one of Paul's friends from the vice squad.

"I think," Keith said solemnly, "that you think I'm drunk."

"No!" the guy standing beside him said. "Perish the thought."

"You sure you're all right?" Paul asked me again.

"All I had was a couple of glasses of wine," I said.

"I don't want the party ruined," Paul said. "I don't want Pop to even hear about this."

"I'll take him home," I said.

"Are you all right to drive?"

"Yeah, sure."

"Maybe you better drive them," the guy from vice said.

"If we're both gone, my father's liable to notice."

"I'll take them, then."

"No, let Allan take him. He's Allan's buddy. Look, I'll tell Pop and his mother that he didn't feel good," Paul said. The guy on vice snorted. "And that you took him home. Pop can take Mrs. Stevens home. You stay with him. See if you can get him to go to bed."

"The evening is still young," Keith said. "Why don't we all go back in the house and have some more champagne?"

There was something funny about it, why I don't know, maybe the way he carefully pronounced each word, and we all laughed. Keith was too drunk to notice that we were laughing at him, not with him, and he actually started to get out of the car. The guy from vice pushed him gently but firmly back in the car.

"You've had all you're going to get, my young friend," he said.

"I don't think I like you," Keith said.

"Gee, I'm sorry to hear about that," the guy from vice said.

"Have you got the keys to this car?" Paul asked Keith.

"Certainly," Keith said. It came out "shertainly."

"Are you going to be a good guy and give them to Allan, so he can drive you home?" Paul asked.

"Anything that Allan wants," Keith said. "You want to take me home, old buddy?"

"Give me the keys," I said. He had a hard time finding them, but finally he put them in my hand.

"Well," Keith said, "it would seem that I owe one and all an apology."

"Forget it," Paul said. "Just let Al take you home. Don't give him any trouble."

"I wouldn't think of it," Keith said.

"For God's sake, drive slow," Paul said. "All we need now is to have you get picked up taking him home from Pop's party for Larry."

"I'll be all right," I said, putting the key in the ignition and starting the engine. I backed out of the driveway. When I stopped to shift into drive, I glanced back at the house. Aunt Rose was there. She was talking to Paul. I didn't, of course, know what Paul was saying to her, but I was relieved. We had gotten out of there just in time.

Keith hummed on the ride to his house. Or he made a noise like humming. If he was humming one song in particular, I had never heard it before. And once he burped. A magnificent burp, from the pit of his stomach, sounding like a bass drum. He turned and smiled at me with pride just as his bad breath reached my nostrils.

"What's with you anyway?" I asked.

"In vino veritas," he said.

"What's that mean?"

"In wine, truth," he said. He giggled. "That's Latin. I can also say 'all Gaul is divided in three parts.' You don't speak Latin?"

"No," I said. "Why did you get plastered?"

"It sneaked up on me when I wasn't looking," he said reasonably.

"Are you going to get sick?"

"As your brother announced to the world in general, I have already been sick," he said. And then a moment later, "Pull over quick! You and the power of suggestion!"

I pulled to the curb and stopped. He pushed the door open and threw up again. It almost made me sick to my stomach.

As soon as he stopped heaving, I told him to close the door, and I drove away.

When we got to his house, he took the keys from me and unlocked the door and walked in ahead of me. He headed for the kitchen. I thought he was going to throw up again, but what he did was go to the refrigerator and get out a bottle of beer.

"Is that a good idea?" I asked. I didn't like the role of being his keeper, but there didn't seem to be much choice.

"Beer settles the stomach," he said, as he twisted the cap off and put the neck to his mouth. "Something about the hops, or something."

He took a couple of swallows, burped again, and then walked out of the kitchen and down the stairs into their basement recreation room, their bar I suppose is what it really is, and slumped in one of the chairs facing the plate-glass windows that looked out on the valley, and on the horizon, at Newark and New York.

I walked in and sat on one of the couches.

"Help yourself to a beer," Keith said.

"I've had enough."

"Don't be self-righteous, buddy," he said. "I can't stand self-righteous people."

"I'm not self-righteous," I said. "I just don't want any more to drink."

"Then why don't you go home?" he suddenly exploded. "Go on, get the hell out of here!"

"My father's coming to get me," I said. "He's bringing your mother home."

He stood up and looked down at me. He was weaving a little. He glowered at first, and then suddenly he started to smile.

"Only kidding," he said. "You know that, don't you?"

"Yeah, I know," I said, and managed a smile back at him.

He turned, staggered, and then, just as I was sure he was going to fall flat on his face, walked out of the basement. I saw him put his hand out to steady himself when he got to the stairs, and then I heard him going up the stairs, heavily.

When he got to the corridor upstairs, the carpet muffled the sound of his feet, and I couldn't hear a thing. I don't know how long I waited, a couple of minutes probably, at least until it occurred to me that he had the keys to the Mercedes and was entirely capable of getting in it and trying to drive. Then I ran up the stairs and down the corridor to the front door. The Mercedes was sitting in the driveway where I'd parked it. I walked upstairs softly, taking them two at a time. The door to his bedroom was open, and he was on the bed, on his back, mouth open, fully dressed, sound asleep.

I saw that the bottle of beer he had had in his hand was on the floor beside his bed, and that most of it had spilled out. I went in his bathroom, got a towel, and mopped it up. Then I looked down at him. He was dead to the world.

I realized that his mother would certainly look in on him when she came home. And if she saw him looking the way he did now, he was in trouble.

So I undressed him, which is a lot harder than it sounds. Keith was a big guy, and he was absolutely limp. Finally, however, I had him down to his underwear and managed to stuff him under the covers. Then I turned off the light and went downstairs. Instead of going back to the recreation room, however, I went in the living room, turned on the TV, and sat down to wait for my father.

I had about two hours to feel sorry for myself. Here I was, baby-sitting a drunk, watching the boob tube, when my brother was having a party at my house. But I was there long enough to stop feeling sorry for myself and to be honest enough with myself to realize that while I was officially a guest at the party, I was actually the little brother, which was the same thing as saying the unpaid maid. Let Paul do some of the cleaning up. I had heard, moreover, some of Paul's and Larry's friends talk about a bachelor party for Larry, and I wondered if I was going to be invited to that, or whether I was going to be considered just the little brother.

And then I remembered Marilyn and the party to which I had been invited because I was a friend of Keith's. I owed him for that. Marilyn was a *stunning* lady. Getting to meet her, to get invited to her party, was worth having to undress Keith and watch the tube.

The truth of the matter is, I fell asleep watching a talk show, and the next thing I knew Mrs. Stevens was shaking my shoulder.

"How's Keith?"

"He's all right," I said. "He went to bed."

"Does he need anything?"

"No, I don't think so."

"Something he ate?" my father said.

"I think so," I said.

"I'd better look in on him," she said.

"He's all right," I said. If she got close, she wouldn't be able to miss the smell of the booze.

"Is there anything I can do, Virginia?" my father asked.

"No, thank you, Paul," she said. "Thanks, anyway."

"Then I'll take this young one home," he said. "I'll see you tomorrow, Virginia."

"I'll look forward to it," Mrs. Stevens said, and she touched my father on the arm.

My father, I could not help but notice, was in a very good mood.

"You better drive," he said. "I've had more than I should have."

"Shame on you," I said, mocking him.

"Your son gets engaged, it's a good reason," he said. "I'm sorry Keith got sick. What did he do, eat everything in sight?"

"I guess," I said.

"Well, no real harm done," my father said. "I'm glad that his getting sick didn't ruin the party for his mother. I think she had a good time."

When we got home, I saw that the house was a mess. Everything had been carried into the kitchen, the plates and ashtrays and things like that, but there was enough of a mess left to make it clear that I was going to spend Saturday morning with a vacuum cleaner in my hand.

Since Aunt Rose wasn't up, Paul and I made breakfast of what we felt like eating, rather than what was supposed to be good for us. There was some hard-crusted bread left, plus what looked like twenty pounds of cold cuts, so we made submarines: white turkey meat, sliced ham, cheese, tomatoes, salami, and some other stuff.

We were both surprised when the door chime went off. I want to answer it, and there was Keith.

"What is that thing in your hand?" he asked cheerfully. "You're not actually going to eat something like that on an empty stomach, are you?"

"Don't knock it until you've tried it," I said. "Come on in." I was surprised to see him at all, much less so cheerful. As drunk as he had been just a few hours before, I would have bet that he would have been sick all day.

He followed me in the house.

"Good morning," Keith said to Paul.

"Well, well," Paul said, more than a little sarcastic, "if it isn't the life of the party! How do you feel, Lushwell?"

"A lot better than I have any right to feel," Keith replied.

"Don't worry about it, kid," Paul said. He was no longer sarcastic. Now he was sympathetic and big-brotherly. "It happens to just about everybody, sooner or later. And no harm was done. You'll feel a lot better if you get something in your stomach. You think you could handle a sandwich?"

It occurred to me right then that Paul wasn't being big-brotherly at all. If I had gotten bombed and thrown up all over the hall bathroom, Paul wouldn't be all sympathy and kind advice. I'd have never heard the end of it, and my brothers could write books on how to make nasty remarks.

"I think I could manage some turkey," Keith graciously announced. "I don't know about the tomatoes and salami."

My big-brotherly big brother made him a white-meat turkey and lettuce sandwich.

As it turned out, he earned it. Without him I would have spent all Saturday and most of Sunday cleaning up the house and returning the chairs and other stuff we had borrowed for the party. With his help and his mother's station wagon, we were through by three that afternoon.

From the way Aunt Rose treated Keith, it was pretty clear that she thought his delicate little tummy had been upset by some of the food he'd eaten, and she was embarrassed that one of my little friends had been poisoned under her roof. There was something obviously unjust about that. It was also pretty obvious that having her think that was better than having her know sweet innocent Keith had gotten bombed.

Anyway, when we came back to the house from returning the folding chairs to the VFW Post, Aunt Rose turned us loose. We went up to his house to watch the end of the ball game on the tube. I was watching the game when suddenly something cold and wet was slapped into my hand. It was a bottle of beer.

"You're a glutton for punishment, aren't you?" I asked.

"I told you last night, it's good for the stomach," he said. "The hops or something."

I didn't want it, but it was easier to take it than it would have been to act like a member of the Springview Temperance League. He had three more before the game was over. He didn't seem to notice, or if he noticed, he didn't seem to care that he was drinking alone.

When the game was over, we watched a rerun of Lucy, and then Mrs. Stevens came in.

"You are going to Marilyn's party, aren't you?" she asked.

"You couldn't keep Al away with a team of horses," Keith said. "He's got a thing for her. I can't imagine why."

"Ignore him," Mrs. Stevens said to me. "There's no other way to deal with him."

"And what are your plans for the evening?" Keith asked.

"We're going to dinner and then to the Papermill Playhouse in Millburn," she said.

"By 'we,' I guess you mean you and Mr. Corelli?" Keith asked.

"Why, yes, I do," she said.

"Remember to drive slow," Keith said. "Or go in Mr. Corelli's car."

It was a bad joke, but we laughed.

"I am going in his car," she said. "Which means that you and Allan will have to be careful, since you'll be in the Mercedes."

"I'd better be going," I said. "It's time for supper."

"But you'll eat the the country club," Mrs. Stevens said. "There's a buffet."

"I didn't know about that," I said.

"Oh, Marilyn goes first class," Keith said somewhat bitterly.

"What else had you planned for tonight?" Mrs. Stevens replied testily. "Sitting around here drinking beer and watching television?"

"I'm going, Mother," Keith said. "I'm going." He got up. "Come on, Al, I'll drive you home."

"Allan, why don't you just take our car, and then pick Keith up?" Mrs. Stevens said.

That made sense, but I don't like to drive other people's cars.

"Go ahead, Al," Keith said. "I'll take a nap for a couple of hours."

That decided it for me. I realized suddenly that I didn't want him to get drunk again tonight, and that his getting drunk again was a real possibility.

"If you're sure it's all right?"

"How many accidents have you had?" Keith asked.

"None, as a matter of fact," I said.

"Well, I'm three up on you. Two fender-bendings and one jolly good one," he said. "The car is obviously safer with you than with me."

"I'll pick you up at seven."

"The orgy is scheduled for seven-thirty," Keith said.

"It's not an orgy, Keith," his mother said.

"Pagan ritual, then," he said.

"If I pick you up at seven, that'll give us half an hour to get there," I said.

"If you're setting your sights on someone like Marilyn," Keith said, "you're going to have to learn that you arrive fashionably late, say eight, and never on time."

CHAPTER 7

Supper was on the table when I got home.

"I'm not going to eat," I told Aunt Rose. "I'm going to a party. There's going to be a buffet."

"If I didn't feel like the orphan of the family," Aunt Rose said, "this would be funny. Your father's going out for dinner. Larry's, naturally, with Barbara. Paul called up and said he has to work. And now you. And look at that table!"

"I'll help you put it away," I said.

My father, fresh from the shower and tieless, came into my room as I was dressing.

"I suspect that you've been helping yourself to my good ties again," he said. "Although I don't know why, I never see you in one." Then he saw that I was wearing a dress shirt. "Big date?"

"Sort of," I said.

"Where's Keith?"

"Home," I said.

"And you've got Mrs. Stevens's fancy car?"

"It was her idea," I said. "She sort of insisted."

"Where are you going?"

"To the country club."

"That's a little rich for your blood, isn't it? I've been wondering if I can afford to join."

"Have you been asked?"

"The mayor told me he thought it would be a good idea if I did."

"I'll let you know if I like it," I said.

"Something special? Or are you just going to see how the other half lives?"

"Both," I said. "Mrs. Stevens's roommate at college has a daughter. She's having a birthday party." I paused. "That's sort of complicated, isn't it?"

"Well, I think it was very nice of Mrs. Stevens to get you an invitation," my father said. He was in my closet, fruitlessly searching for his necktie.

"It's not here," he said. "Where is it?"

"The last time I counted, I had two brothers, both of whom wear neckties."

"Larry," he said. "I saw him wearing it."

"You could give it to him as a wedding present," I said.

"Have a good time," he said.

"You, too," I said.

"What makes you think I'm going out?" He was a little embarrassed.

"Mrs. Stevens told me. Dinner and the theater."

"Why not, Allan?" my father said very seriously. "We're both alone."

"I'm all for it," I said. "I think she's great."

"Nothing serious, of course," my father said. "You know. Dinner. A few laughs. This is the first time in twenty years I've had my evenings free. The trouble with fighting crime is that the bad guys generally do their thing late at night."

"On Christmas Eve," I added.

He smiled at me. "Speaking of crime," he said, "try to remember not to beat up anybody tonight."

"I thought we had agreed not to talk about that."

"Sorry," he said, and walked out of the room. Then he came back in and handed me twenty dollars.

"What's this for?" I asked.

"In case the girl gets fresh, you can take a taxi home," he said. Then he added. "You worked like hell for the party, and I appreciate it. Have a good time, Allan."

I got to Keith's house at seven-ten. He wasn't dressed. I saw that Mrs. Stevens was all ready to go, and my father wasn't due for twenty minutes. I sat around the living room with her while Keith took a shower. He was one of those guys who sings in the shower, and it was sort of funny hearing his voice.

My father arrived right on time, and I remembered what Keith had said about being fashionably late when dealing with the upper crust. Mrs. Stevens didn't seem at all upset that he was right on time; it looked to me as if she was highly pleased.

And he looked pleased to see me.

"I'm glad you're still here," he said. "If I can catch a ride with you, Virginia—"

"Certainly," she said.

"Then Allan can take my car."

"That's not necessary," Mrs. Stevens said. "We have more than enough cars."

"We don't want the two of them attracting Officer Lawton's attention, do we?" my father said.

So we drove to the country club in my father's car. Like many people who spend a lot of time working in cars, I suppose, or maybe like most cops, my father is not impressed with cars as status symbols. The only difference between his car and a police car was that his didn't say "Police Department" on the doors. It was a stock Ford, with the big engine, black sidewall tires, and an extra antenna for the police radio. Stuck to the dashboard was a blue blinker. When he had to, all he had to do was jerk it loose and put it on the roof. It had a magnetic base. And there was a whooper too, hidden behind the grill. Switches on the dashboard turned them on and off.

I guess this made an impression on me because of the difference—the vinyl instead of leather—between my father's car and the Mercedes Mrs. Stevens had loaned me to go home.

Anyway we got what I thought was a dirty look when we walked up in front of the door of the country club. The doorman, a guy about my age, had seen us drive past to the parking lot and thought we were a couple of cops.

"What can I do for you?" he asked.

"Point us in the direction of the Withers orgy," Keith said.

"You're guests?"

"No, as a matter of fact," Keith said, "I'm a member."

I had another one of those thoughts that seem to get me in trouble the minute we walked inside. The country club looked like a funeral home with a bar and an orchestra. I don't really know what I expected, maybe a large room with crystal chandeliers and people in formal clothing waltzing to the music of a string orchestra, but what I got was the Blue Room, apparently because of the blue wallpaper, full of people my age, some of them actually dressed in blue jeans and sweatshirts.

There was a line just inside the door, and I found myself following Keith in it. Mrs. Withers was there, and a tall, heavy-set man with a mustache in a dinner jacket, and Marilyn. Marilyn was wearing a yellow dress, a long one, with bare shoulders. She was everything I had remembered, and more.

Mrs. Withers kissed Keith on the cheek.

"Oh, you look so nice, Keith," she said. "Which is more than I can say for some people."

"Mother!" Marilyn protested.

"Happy birthday, Goofus," Keith said to Marilyn.

"And you, too, Allan," Mrs. Withers said to me, and shook my hand.

"Happy birthday," I said to Marilyn, and she shook my hand.

"Daddy," Marilyn said. "This is Allan Corelli."

"How are you, Allan?" he said. He shook my hand and gave me sort of a vague smile.

And then we were inside. There was a small band, five or six guys in far-out purple and bright blue tuxedoes wtih lace shirt fronts and lace cuffs, playing loudly in one corner. At one end of the room was a bar, and I wasn't at all surprised to see Keith head straight for it.

It was a beer and champagne bar, no hard liquor, and when I asked the bartender for champagne and got a funny look, I realized that the beer was supposed to be for the boys and the champagne for the girls. I hadn't been in the place sixty seconds and already had made my first social goof.

I then followed Keith to the buffet.

"Look," he said, "breakfast."

I had to laugh. The buffet table held the same stuff—turkey, ham, even salami—that we had eaten for breakfast and that Aunt Rose had laid out earlier.

Keith, who hadn't spoken to anybody in the place so far, filled a plate with cold cuts. I did the same and then followed him to sit in chairs lining one wall.

Then people came to speak to him. While he wasn't actually nasty, he wasn't exactly friendly, either. He introduced me to fifteen or twenty people, who didn't seem particularly interested in meeting me.

I was asked if I was at Saint Whatsisname's, the school he'd gone to, with Keith, and when I said no, that seemed to exhaust all the possibilities for polite conversation. I remember looking around for Marilyn and seeing her surrounded by half a dozen guys. And then I guess I just glazed over.

This party wasn't much different from the kind of parties we'd had in Newark. The only real difference was that it was being held in the country club, and that I hadn't grown up with these kids.

Sometime later I sort of woke up and realized that I was sitting all by myself. When I looked around, I could see Keith at the bar, surrounded by maybe six people, and Marilyn at the buffet, surrounded by the same number of guys.

I got up, walked over to the bar, and overheard enough of Keith's conversation to understand that it was about people and places I'd never heard of. The bartender filled my champagne glass again, and after standing on the edge of the people around

Keith for a couple of minutes, I went back to the wall.

I put my arm on the back of the chair and gave myself a pain-ful whack on the elbow from a doorknob I hadn't seen before. There was a door in the wall, and the reason I hadn't noticed it was because I wasn't supposed to. It had been designed to look like part of the wall.

Curiosity got the better of me. I reached for the knob and turned it and pushed the door open a crack. There was enough light in the room from outside lights for me to see that it held four pool tables, *billiards* tables, the kind without pockets.

I thought about it a minute. It really wasn't a very polite thing for me to do, but so would leaving be impolite. If I had been alone, I would have been long gone, but Keith was with me and he looked like he was having a good time and wouldn't want to check out. He couldn't anyway, without hurting Marilyn's feel-ings. When I looked at it that way, it seemed to be the right, maybe even the polite, thing to do.

A guy sitting around alone puts a chill on a party.

I stood up, looked around the room, and when no one was looking, slipped between two of the chairs and through the door. I quickly closed it behind me. I looked around the billiards room, found the main door to it, and walked over. Sure enough there was a plate of light switches. I flipped them on one at a time and finally got the one I needed, a large, hooded fixture over the closest pool table. I shut the others off.

There was a rack of cues on one wall, and I found one that seemed to fit right. Now there was only one problem. I didn't know how to shoot billiards. Pool, or pocket pool, was something else. I play a fair game of pool. But this was something new.

I took the plastic cover off the table and looked at what I had. There were two cue balls, or at least two white balls. One of them had black spots on it, and the other was plain. There was also a red ball. And of course, there were no pockets to knock them in, just cushions around the four sides of the table.

I remembered then that this kind of pool was called "Three Cushion."

I took off my jacket, put it on the next table, and loosened my necktie. Then I picked up the cue, chalked it, hit the spotted cue ball into the red ball, and counted as the cue ball continued to bounce off cushions. My cue ball hit four cushions easily, and it looked like if I hit it harder, I could hit five or six. So that wasn't the way the game was played—that was too easy.

Then I tried counting the cushions the red ball bounced off after I hit it with the cue ball. Same thing. If I hit it hard enough, I could bounce it off six cushions, maybe more.

Then I decided that maybe it meant you had to bounce the cueball off three cushions before hitting the red ball. I missed the first couple of times I tried, but then I got the knack, and sort of laughing at myself I decided that I was either the world's greatest billiards player or was still doing it wrong.

Then I decided that the other cueball, the one without the spots, was probably involved. You were probably supposed to bounce your cue ball off three cushions and then hit both the other balls.

When I tried this, it took me about six shots before I did it the first time, and even after that, I was able to do it only about once in three times. I then decided that I was close, but that there was probably one more rule. You had to hit three cushions, then the red ball, and finally the other cue ball.

After maybe fifteen minutes I decided that this must be the way to play billiards; I couldn't think of anything else to do with the three balls. I could do this about once in five shots. With practice, I'd probably get better.

The trouble with playing this way was leaving the cue ball in a position where you could shoot again and have any chance at all of making the shot. Sometimes it just lined up easily, but most of the time, the way the balls stopped on the table, the world's greatest pool shark couldn't have bounced his cue ball off three cushions and then hit the red ball and the other cue ball.

"What in the world are you doing?" the voice about two feet behind me said. I almost dropped the cue. I turned and found myself looking at Marilyn.

"Uh—" I said, in perfect control of the situation. "I'm . . . uh . . . shooting a little pool."

She chuckled. "I can see that, dummy," she said. "I mean, why did you try to carom off the red? In the corner you could never make it."

"Carom?"

"Bounce," she said.

"Oh," I said.

"Have you ever played three cushion before?" Marilyn asked.

"No," I confessed.

"But that isn't the first cue you've ever held, is it?" she asked. "I've been watching."

"I guess I shouldn't have come in here, huh?" I asked.

"Give me the cue," she said. I handed it to her. She bent over the table, stroked the spotted cue ball into a corner, where it bounced off onto the other cue ball, onto another cushion, and then into the red ball.

"*That's* the way it's done," Marilyn said, and walked to the other side of the table. She lined up on the spotted cue ball again.

"You didn't hit three cushions first," I protested. "And you hit the other cue ball before you hit the red one."

"So?" she asked, and shot again, this time shooting into one cushion, then bouncing off the red ball, into a corner, and finally into the spotless cue ball.

"That's two to zero," she said.

"You didn't bounce it off the cushions first," I said again.

"Oh," she said. "What did you do, make up your own rules?"

"I had to," I said.

"There are four ways to score," she said, and explained them to me. They all made sense, and I felt like a dummy for not being able to figure them out myself.

"Come on," she said. "We'll play a game."

She showed me how the game started by bouncing the ball off the far cushion to see how close you could roll it to the near cushion. This was called "lagging." The one who came closest got the choice of cue ball (spotted or spotless) and could either shoot first or make the loser break to start the game.

Six or seven shots into the game I gathered my courage.

"Look," I said, "I really appreciate this."

"What?"

"You not saying anything about me ducking out of your party and trying to save my feelings by playing with me."

"There were a lot of bored people in there," she said. "Only one of whom had the guts to do anything about it. Now there are two. Okay?"

"You're bored with your own party?"

She had been bent over the table. Now she straightened up and leaned on her cue.

"This isn't *my* party, really," she said. "It's my mother's party for me. You understand?" She didn't wait for a reply. "So I acted happy and pleased while she and Daddy were in there. But when they left—they're having a dinner for a bunch of their friends in the dining room—I decided I'd really rather see what you were doing in here. All right?"

"Yeah, sure," I said. Then my mouth ran away with me. "You're really something special," I said.

"Why, thank you, sir," she said, and she stuck her index finger under her chin and did a little curtsy. It was even funnier since she was hanging onto the pool cue with her other hand.

Then she bent over the pool table and made her shot.

It was about fifteen or twenty minutes later, I guess, that we heard the crash. Something wooden broke, and then there was a large thump against the wall with the door we'd come through.

"I'll bet I know who's responsible for that," she said. She laid her cue on the table and ran toward the door. I ran after her, beat her to it, and pulled the door inward. Keith was in the middle of the room, his fists raised, in a fighting crouch, nearly facing me. I looked to my left and saw what had caused the noise. A guy was trying to untangle himself from the rows of chairs against the wall.

"That's a boy," Keith said. "Get up and I'll give it to you again!"

"Oh, damn!" Marilyn said, behind me.

I went to Keith. He pushed me aside.

"I don't need your help this time, ol' buddy," he said. "Just stay out of the way."

The guy tangled up in the chairs finally got to his feet and started for Keith. I was behind Keith, and I wrapped my arms around him. He struggled, but I'm strong, and more importantly I was sober. He couldn't get away. The guy he had apparently pushed (or for that matter, thrown—at least two of the chairs were broken) had his fists balled.

"You hit him," I said to him, "and I'll tear your head off!"

It sounds far more heroic than it was. He wasn't a little guy, but he was a lot smaller than Keith and me. He didn't lose any face by not hitting Keith, and a couple of his friends made it even better for him by grabbing him.

And when that happened Keith stopped trying to get away from me. He relaxed.

"What the hell happened?" I asked.

"Let me go, Al Capone," he said. "I'm all right."

"What happened?"

"I'll tell you later," he said. "Let's get out of here."

"Thanks a lot, Keith," Marilyn said, angry, sarcastic. "I knew I could count on you."

"Happy birthday, Goofus," Keith said. And then he marched out of the place.

I looked down at her and shrugged my shoulders, and then trotted after him. I really felt like tearing his head off. Things had turned out even better than I had hoped. I had had Marilyn all to myself, despite the guys who had known her for years, and now my drunken buddy was leaving the party about thirty seconds before we could get thrown out.

When I turned at the door to look at Marilyn, I saw her father coming quickly into the room. Well, I thought, I'm really making a good impression on her father. When I got outside, I saw Keith walking toward where I'd parked. There didn't seem to be any point in running to catch up with him, so I stopped running and just walked.

I guess I was twenty yards from where Keith was leaning against the fender of the Ford when I heard footsteps behind me. I turned, and it was Marilyn.

"Hey," she said.

"Hey, yourself."

"Do *you* have to go?" she asked.

"You know the rule," I said, trying to make a joke of it. "The one you take to the prom is the one you take home from the prom."

"I suppose," she said, and laughed. "Well, anyway, thanks a lot."

"For what?"

"For keeping the mess from getting worse," she said.

"It runs in the family," I said.

"You're pretty special yourself," she said, and then she really stunned me. She popped up on her toes and kissed me. Then she started back to the country club building.

"Hey!" I called.

"Yeah?"

"Can I call you?"

"You'd better," she said, and waved at me.

That was enough to put me in the mood to forgive Keith for anything.

CHAPTER 8

I didn't say anything to Keith when I got to Pop's car. I just unlocked the door, got in, and reached across and unlocked his side. He got in beside me.

"I seem to have underestimated you," he said. "You really do sweep them off their feet, don't you?"

"Aw, come on!"

"Where did you vanish to with her?" he asked. "I looked around and the both of you were gone."

"We were shooting pool," I said. "What was the fight about?"

"Shooting *pool?*"

"You know, you hit the little balls with a stick," I said. "*Pool.*"

"Oh, sure. You and W. C. Fields."

"What was the fight about?"

"Thanks for stopping it when you did," he said. "As mad as I was I might have hurt him."

"What was it about?"

"Not now, ol' buddy," he said. "Let's go get a beer somewhere. I know a place in Millburn."

"In Pop's car? Don't be silly."

"Go by my place and I'll get the station wagon," he said.

"We'll go by your place, period," I said. "Since you got us thrown out of the party, I'm going home."

"I didn't get us thrown out, I left," he said.

"Just in time."

"Let's go get a beer," he said. "It's too early to go home."

"That's the way the ball bounces, ol' buddy," I said.

"Okay," he said. "Have it your way."

He didn't say one more word all the way to his house, and when we got there, he jumped out of the car without a word. I shrugged my shoulders and started home.

I'd gone about four blocks when a car caught up with me, crawled up to my bumper, and started blowing the horn. When I passed under the street lights at the next intersection, there was enough light for me to see in the rearview mirror that it was Keith driving his mother's yellow Mercedes coupe.

I pulled to the curb and he pulled parallel beside me and rolled down the window.

"Come on," he said. "Let's go get a beer. Drop your father's car off at the house."

"Every time I go someplace with you, you start punching people out," I said. "I'm going home."

"In that case," he said cheerfully, "go to hell." And then he raced off, laying rubber. To tell the truth I felt guilty, or maybe disloyal. He was my pal. I should have gone with him. Probably, if it hadn't been for Marilyn, I would have gone with him. But I was in a mood to think about her, not about keeping Keith out of a fight.

Thinking about Marilyn was very pleasant. While I was interested in the ladies, you might even say a student of the subject, the truth was that I had studied them from a distance. When it got down to talking with them, it generally turned out that we had very little to say to each other. There seemed to be a sort of Corelli's Law: the better they looked, the less we had to talk about. And generally, too, they hung around in pairs or trios, and I usually got the idea that they were somehow laughing at me.

Marilyn seemed to be the exception that proved the rule. Not only did she not have a girl friend at her elbow all the time, but I could talk to her easily. And as I said before, she was stunning. Even shooting pool she was one good-looking female.

I watched the tube awhile in bed and finally turned it off and went to sleep.

And then, all at once, my bedroom door opened and the light in the ceiling snapped on. My father was standing there.

"What's the matter?"

"Boy, am I glad to see you," he said. "There's been an accident. Virginia just called. Keith's been in a wreck. You want to come along?"

He didn't wait for a reply. He was gone even before I jumped out of bed and pulled on a pair of jeans and a sweater and ran barefoot down the stairs after him carrying a pair of sneakers in my hand.

"Get in the back," he said, "we're going to pick up Mrs. Stevens."

"What happened?" I asked as he backed out of the driveway. I've never seen my father lay rubber. That's not saying he doesn't drive fast when he's in a hurry, just that he knows what he's doing. And he was too busy at first to talk to me. He didn't even reply.

"What kind of a car was Keith driving? The station wagon?"

"That little Mercedes," I said. "The coupe."

My father got on the radio.

"Six-six," he said.

"Go ahead, six-six," the Springview operator replied.

"Get on the horn to Newark Traffic and see what you can find out about an accident an hour or so ago involving a yellow Mercedes coupe and get back to me."

"Ten-four, six-six," the radio operator said.

A couple of minutes later we rolled to the curb in front of Keith's house. Mrs. Stevens was standing on the sidewalk waiting for us. My father reached across the seat and opened the door for her. As she got in, he pulled the blue flasher loose from the dashboard and put it on the roof and turned it on.

"What happened, Allan?" Mrs. Stevens asked me.

"Al was in bed," my father answered for me. "He doesn't know any more about it than I do. I've got a call into Newark Traffic."

"Presbyterian Hospital called and told me Keith had been in an accident. That's all they'd tell me," she said. Bitterly she added, "I think what they really wanted to know was if someone was going to pay the bill."

"Now take it easy," my father said. "Don't go looking for bad news. If it was serious, they would have told you." He picked up the microphone again.

"Six-six at South Orange at Gregory, heading for Presbyterian Hospital," he said.

"Ten-four, six-six," the operator said.

We were going pretty fast, but Pop wasn't running stoplights, and he didn't have the whooper on. The flasher was just to let any patrol cars who happened to see him doing twenty-five miles over the speed limit know it was a cop.

"Six-six," the radio said.

"Go ahead."

"Newark Traffic reports a two-car collision involving a yellow Mercedes and a Ford at Raymond Boulevard and Second Street. Two hospitalized, both at Presbyterian. The Ford ran a stop sign. Investigation officers have requested a blood sample. Citizen named Waldron, Thomas T., forty-five-year-old white male."

"Anything on the other driver?"

"Stevens, Keith. White male, seventeen."

"Anything on his condition?"

"Probably broken leg," the radio operator said matter-of-factly.

"Oh, my God!" Mrs. Stevens said.

"Okay," my father said. "Six-six is enroute to Presbyterian, in case I'm needed."

"Ten-four, six-six."

When we pulled into the emergency entrance of Presbyterian Hospital, the security officer on duty, probably because of the blue light on the roof of the car, pointed to a parking space marked with a sign, "Official Visitors." We got out of the car and walked into the hospital.

A weary-looking intern told my father that Keith was in the treatment room, and that if we wanted, we could wait. He couldn't tell us anything about Keith's condition.

But when we got to the seventh floor, a middle-aged, gray-haired nurse, the kind who would be calm if the wall had just fallen in, told us that Keith had been taken to a room on the fifth floor.

Mrs. Stevens sort of sagged against my father and started to sniffle as we walked back to the elevators with his arm around her. On the fifth floor another nurse gave us the room number. When we pushed the door open, Keith was in bed. He looked gray. One leg was in a cast from the ankle almost to the middle. The cast was outside the covers. He had a couple of Band-Aids on his face, one on his forehead, and another on his chin, near the lip.

"He just came around a moment ago," the nurse who had been sitting on a chair against the wall said, getting up and walking over to us. "He's still pretty groggy."

"How bad is it?" Mrs. Stevens asked, walking over to the bed and looking down at him.

"I don't really know, except that he's in no real danger," the nurse said. "You'll have to ask the doctor."

Keith half woke up, groaned a little, and threw up over the side of the bed.

"Oh, damn!" the nurse said. "I was afraid of that."

She started to clean up the mess, and Mrs. Stevens asked her where the doctor was.

"He said he would look in on him in a few minutes," the nurse said.

The smell of the room was too much for me. I went back in the corridor, and even there it was all I could do to keep from tossing my cookies. My father stayed in the room with Keith. A couple of minutes later a man in surgical greens came down the corridor, wiping his sweaty forehead, and walked into the room. I got up and went in after him.

Keith was awake. Groggy, but awake.

"Hey, ol' buddy," he said, when he saw me.

The doctor looked in his eyes and listened to his heart and

then motioned for all of us to follow him out into the corridor.

"There has been a good deal of damage to the knee," he said, without saying anything else first. "I think we fixed it. He'll be in the cast five, six weeks. I'll be able to tell better tomorrow, when we get some pictures of it. There's some pain, and I've given orders that he be given something for it. So the only logical thing for you to do is go home and get some sleep."

"Can't I stay with him?" Mrs. Stevens asked.

"I can't forbid you to, of course," the doctor said. "But it really wouldn't serve any purpose. He'll be out like a light until seven-thirty, eight o'clock in the morning."

"We'll take you home, Virginia," my father said. "And Allan will be at your house at six-thirty in the morning to bring you back here."

"I guess that's the only thing to do," she said.

"He's in no danger," the doctor repeated.

"Thank you, Doctor," my father said, and took her arm and started her toward the elevators.

"I think they expect you at the business office," the doctor called after us.

"My God!" Mrs. Stevens said to Pop. "At a time like this! Can't they wait?"

"If they wait, they sometimes don't get their money," my father said. "And somebody has to pay for all this."

"Oh, you're right, of course," she said. "I'm sorry."

Filling out the forms took about five minutes, and then we walked back through the emergency entrance and got back in the car. Pop unstuck the blue flasher from the roof, put it back against the dashboard, and fiddled with the radio.

"Newark Central," he said. "This is Springview six-six."

"Go ahead, Springview six-six."

"Patch me through to the watch officer in Traffic," Pop ordered.

"Hold one," the radio operator said, and then, "Traffic, Lieutenant Loeber."

"Kenny, this is Al Corelli," Pop said.

"Hey, Chief, how are you? What can I do for you?"

"There was a wreck about two hours ago at Raymond Boulevard and Second."

"Yeah. Wiped out a fancy yellow Mercedes."

"Any charges been filed?"

"Yeah. They filed DWI against the driver of the Ford. His blood test showed he was plastered."

"Thanks, Kenny," my father said.

"Anytime, Chief," the watch officer in Traffic said.

"Newark Central, this is Springview six-six clear," my father said, and put the microphone down.

"Okay," he said to Mrs. Stevens. "So now we know most importantly that Keith's going to be all right, and we know the accident wasn't his fault."

"What does DWI mean? What that man said?" she asked.

"Driving while intoxicated," my father said. "He was apparently drunk and ran the stop sign and hit Keith. It could have been much, much worse."

Then he started the engine and we left the hospital. Halfway back home he pulled off Springview Avenue into a McDonald's parking lot.

"I can use a cup of coffee," he said. "I think maybe you can too, Virginia, and I know the bottomless stomach here can eat a burger or something."

We had just carried the tray to a table when Paul came in. It was less of a coincidence than it might seem. Springview Avenue was the route from Newark home. Paul is a cop. Cops never stop looking for something, anything. He had spotted Pop's car. It was as simple as that.

"I'm much too cruddy for a high-class group like this," Paul
said. "Allan, go get me a fried-egg sandwich and a cup of coffee
while I wash up."

By the time I got the food for him, he was back at the table.
He was wearing a nylon zipper jacket, and it was dirty. He
looked, I thought, like he'd just come off the midnight stevedore
shift at the docks. As it happened that wild guess wasn't far off.

"I had a lovely night," he was saying when I sat down. "Root-
ing around the hold of a stinking freighter. Somebody tipped
the feds it was carrying grass."

"Find any?" my father asked.

"Not an ounce," Paul said. "So what brings you to this palace
of culinary artistry at this time of night?"

"There's been an accident," my father said. "A DWI ran a
stop sign and clobbered Keith pretty badly."

"Oh, I'm sorry!" Paul said. "He all right?"

"He's got a pretty badly banged-up knee," my father said. "We
just came from the hospital."

"You weren't hurt, huh, Allan?" Paul asked me.

"I wasn't with him," I said.

"What about that?" my father asked. "How come he was
alone?"

"I dropped him off at the house after the party," I said. "Then
I went home. I guess he went out by himself."

"Why?" Mrs. Stevens asked. There was no way I could answer
that question.

"Did he say where he was going?" Mrs. Stevens asked.

"Uh uh," I said. "Maybe he was hungry and went out for something to eat."

"To Newark?" Paul asked, his voice making it pretty clear I
had made a dumb guess.

"I don't know," I said.

"Well, be thankful only one of them got hurt," my father said. "Paul, if you're headed home, take Allan with you, will you?"

"Yeah, sure."

"I'll have one of the patrol cars pick me up in the morning," my father said. "Allan, take my car and bring Mrs. Stevens to the hospital first thing. Pick her up about six-thirty, okay?"

"Yes, sir," I said.

"They picked up those kids who were burglarizing the houses on the hill," my father said to Paul. "I told the detectives to let them cool their heels in a cell overnight. And I want to be there when they question them first thing in the morning."

"You're supposed to be a chief now, Pop," Paul said. "Chiefs get to sleep late on Sunday mornings. Monday mornings too, come to think of it."

"Women work from sun to sun," Pop replied, "but a policeman's work is never done."

"Paul, that's awful!" Mrs. Stevens said, but she smiled.

Paul was driving a Pontiac Gran Prix. I knew it had probably belonged to some junk dealer—drug dealer. The way it works is that when they catch a drug dealer with illegal narcotics in his car, the car is forfeited. If the car is in good shape, the courts usually turn it over to the police. They make fine undercover cars for detectives—better than the stripped Fords or Chevies the city buys on bids. The detectives and plainclothes guys use them for a while, or until they start to wear out, and then the city sells them at auction.

"This is new," I said, when I got in beside him.

"A little gift from the feds," Paul replied. "Part payment for us helping them on these damned ship searches." Then without pausing for breath he went on. "About midnight tonight I went downtown to get us something to eat. I could have sworn I saw that yellow Mercedes in front of a beer joint on Mott Street."

"Oh?"

"I was tempted to go in and throw you two out on your ear," Paul said. "But I figured, what the hell, you're my little brother. I'd warn you one time, and then break your arm the next time it happened."

"I told you, I wasn't with him," I said. "And how do you know it was the Stevens's Mercedes?"

"How many do you think there are? With one of those St. Something school decals in the window?"

"I told you, Paul, I was home in bed."

"Lucky for you," he said. "You could be in the hospital."

"The other guy was drunk," I said. "They already charged him with DWI."

"How did Pop get involved?" Paul asked. "Your pal use his name?"

"The hospital called Mrs. Stevens. I guess she called Pop."

"You think they got something going?" Paul asked.

"I don't know. It wouldn't bother me if they did," I said.

"How about your pal?" Paul asked.

"I don't know. Why should it?"

"Maybe he doesn't like it. Maybe that's why he's boozing it up."

"What makes you think he's boozing it up?"

"Try not to show your stupidity so much," Paul said. "That guy's trouble, looking for a disaster."

"Ah, get off it, Paul."

"He use grass too, or is booze his thing?"

"Will you cut it out?"

"I don't want either you or Pop in a mess because of him," Paul said.

"Pop can take care of himself, and so can I," I said.

"I made up my mind to tell you, and I told you," Paul said. "Leave it at that."

We didn't say anything else all the way home.

There was a change of plans. Just as soon as my alarm went off, at five minutes after six, my father came in my room.

"Mrs. Stevens is coming here," he announced. "She's going to leave her station wagon for you. I'm going to the hospital with her. You meet her there about eight, eight-thirty. Give her a little company. Stick with her. Drive her where she wants to go. I guess you'd better ask her if she wants to see the wreck. I'll find out where it was towed."

I lay back down for a couple of minutes, but couldn't fall asleep, so I got up and got dressed and went down and got the Sunday paper off the lawn.

Keith and his mother's car had made the front page. There was a four-column picture of the wreck, showing the Mercedes shoved off the road.

"Keith Stevens, 17, of 1140 Mountainbrook Drive, Springview, was hospitalized with leg injuries following a collision at Raymond Blvd. and Second Street at 2:25 this morning. Thomas T. Waldron, 45, driver of the Ford, of 350 Weequahic Ave., was charged by police with running a stop sign and drunken driving."

Larry came in the dining room and read the front page over my shoulder.

"I thought you were with him last night," he said. "How bad is he hurt?"

"His knee is pretty bad," I said. "They have him in a cast from his ankle all the way up."

"Brother Waldron has his you-know-what in a crack," Larry offered. "More than usual, I mean. The DA's on an anti-drunk-driver kick."

"Isn't he always?"

"Sometimes more than others," Larry said tolerantly. "Like before an election."

"Oh."

Larry pushed open the door to the kitchen and dialed a number on the yellow phone that hangs on the wall.

"This is Lieutenant Corelli," he said. It was the first time I'd heard him use his new title. "There was a DWI wreck last night involving a guy named Stevens. The victim, not the drunk. I can't have anything to do with it. The victim's my little brother's buddy. You have someone who can take it?"

When he came back in, I asked, "What was that all about?"

"They call it speedy justice," Larry said. "Brother Waldron's going to go straight from the hospital to court. We'll seek a true bill from the Grand Jury just as soon as we can get it. Which means the DA will want the investigation done yesterday. And obviously I have to keep my hands off." He changed the subject. "Where's Paul? And where did Pop go?"

"Pop went to the hospital with Mrs. Stevens," I said. "And Paul was working with the feds on a narc search last night. I don't think he'll be getting up any time soon."

"I saw the Pontiac," Larry said. "Nice. How long's he had it?"

"Brand new, I think."

"Crime does pay, huh?" Larry said. "I'll have to see if I can beat him out of it."

CHAPTER 9

At almost exactly eight-thirty I was walking across the lobby of Presbyterian Hospital to the elevators when someone called my name. I turned and saw Marilyn and her parents coming out of the gift and florist's shop. Marilyn was carrying a potted plant with three round white flowers.

She was in blue jeans and a shirt, but she looked as good to me then as she had all dressed up the night before.

"Good morning," I said.

"I don't have to ask, I suppose, what you're doing here," Mrs.

Withers said to me as Marilyn's father shook my hand very formally. "Do you know how he is?"

"He's got a pretty badly banged-up knee," I said.

"You weren't with him?" Marilyn asked. I shook my head no.

"We saw it in the paper and came right away," Mrs. Withers said. "Do you know where he is?"

"On the fifth floor," I said.

"Is his mother with him?"

"Yes, ma'am," I said.

Marilyn handed me the potted plant, and we walked to the elevators. There was a velvet-covered chain barring the way, and a security guard at a little desk. He took one look at us and could tell what we were.

"I'm sorry," he said, "visiting hours are ten to twelve in the morning."

"I'm Alton Withers," Marilyn's father said. "I'm a trustee of this hospital."

"In that case," the security guard said, getting to his feet, "I'm sure it will be all right."

I guess I was a little impressed. I'd never met a hospital trustee before. I was even more impressed when we got to the fifth floor. The nurse on duty there, a middle-aged woman with an air of authority, took one look at him, got up, and smiled and addressed him by name.

"Good morning, Mr. Withers," she said. "How can I help you?"

"We're here to see the Stevens boy," he said.

"He's in 523," she said. "And doing very well too, I'm glad to say."

She pushed the door open and Mrs. Withers sort of ran into the room. She went to Mrs. Stevens and hugged her and said, "Ginny, we came just as soon as we saw it in the paper. You really should have called."

Keith was wide awake. The bed had been cranked up, and he was wearing regular pajamas instead of the dresslike thing he'd been wearing the night before. There were some bags under his eyes, he looked a little pale, and his chin, where he had one of the Band-Aids, looked red. But other than that, he looked all right.

"Flowers for little me?" he said. "Oh, Alphonso, you shouldn't have!"

"They're from the Withers, stupid," I said.

Mrs. Withers went to the bed and bent down and kissed him. He grimaced.

"How are you, Keith?" Mr. Withers asked, man-to-man, shaking his hand.

"Aside from this," Keith said, rapping his knuckles on his cast, "just fine, thank you. What do you say, Goofus?"

"You are all right?" Marilyn asked.

"What happened, son?" Mr. Withers asked.

"Well, there I was, minding my own business," Keith said, "and the next thing I knew, there's this strange lady looking down at me and asking if I'm awake."

"You didn't see the man who hit you?" Mr. Withers asked.

"No, sir."

"Well, according to the paper," Mr. Withers said, "he was drunk and ran a stop sign."

"Well, I guess that explains a lot," Keith said.

"They've got to get the drunken driver off the streets," Mr. Withers said. "That's all there is to it."

I remembered what Larry had told me an hour before about the guy who had hit Keith going straight from the hospital to court. But I didn't say anything.

"Well," Mr. Withers said, "you'll be out of here in no time, Keith."

"By one this afternoon," Keith said. "Just as soon as the doctor shows up."

"So soon?" Mr. Withers asked.

"I had Dr. Furman come in," Mrs. Stevens said. "He went over the X rays, and he said there's no reason to keep him here. He can lie in bed just as well at home."

"Well, good," Mr. Withers said.

"And we won't even have to buy or rent crutches," Mrs. Stevens said. "Paul says that his VFW Post—"

"Paul?" Mr. Withers asked.

"Mr. Corelli," Mrs. Stevens said. It looked to me as if she blushed a little. "Allan's father."

"Certainly, I should have known," Mr. Withers said.

"Well, apparently the VFW keeps a stock of supplies like that to loan as a public service. He said to ask you, Allan, if you would go to get a set."

"Yes, ma'am," I said. "I'll go right now."

"Can I go with you?" Marilyn asked.

"Sure."

"Don't you want to stay here, dear, and visit with Keith?" her mother said.

"I visited with Keith last night, at my party, Mother," Marilyn replied innocently. "Can't I go with Al?"

"Of course you can, Kitten," Mr. Withers said.

"Be careful," Keith called from the bed. "It's dangerous out there."

In the corridor I was unable to resist the temptation to meow at Marilyn.

"Very funny, wiseguy," she said. "Well that was really hypocrisy honed to a fine degree, wasn't it?"

"What do you mean?"

"At seven-fifteen Daddy was coaching Mother on all the things she was to say to Keith's mother about Keith's lousy behavior at the party. They could hardly wait until it was a 'decent' time to call her up. Then I brought the paper in. Instantly old bad-manners-the-bully became poor-dear-Keith, the innocent little lamb."

I looked at her and said nothing. Then I raised my hand to push the down button at the elevator. I suddenly realized the hand was occupied; Marilyn's hand was in it. We let go of each other, I pushed the button, in a couple of seconds the elevator arrived, and we got on it. I pushed the lobby button and then decided to push my luck. I put my arm around Marilyn's shoulders.

"Watch it, Romeo," she said. "It's only quarter to nine in the morning."

But she didn't pull away from me until the door opened onto the lobby.

We went out and got in the Stevens's station wagon and started for downtown and Norton P. Silver Post 2378, VFW. Silver had been a Newark cop who had gone in the Army during World War II and become an MP. He'd gotten killed as a military police-man in the Battle of the Bulge, and they named the VFW Post, most of whose members were either cops or firemen or men who worked around the courthouse, after him.

"What was the fight about at your party?" I asked.

Marilyn didn't answer, so I asked her again. "What was Keith fighting about at your party?"

"Is it important?" she asked.

It wasn't, obviously. But I wondered why she didn't want to talk about it.

"Yeah, I think it is," I said.

"Nothing out of the ordinary," Marilyn said. "Somebody said

something Keith didn't like, so Keith hit him."

"What did somebody say that Keith didn't like?" I pursued.

"You won't give up, will you?" Marilyn asked. "Okay, you asked for it. Walter—the boy Keith threw into the chairs—made some cracks about you and Keith."

"What kind of a crack?"

"It wasn't very nice, okay?" she said. "Leave it at that."

"No. Guessing about what somebody said about me is worse than knowing."

She shrugged her shoulders. "Somebody asked who you were. Somebody said you were from Newark."

"So?"

"Walter said something about not being surprised, that Keith had worn out all his friends, and that it wasn't surprising he was down to running around with a, a not very nice name for Italians, from the city."

"What was the not very nice name?"

"He called you a dago," Marilyn said. "That's when Keith grabbed him."

I laughed. It wasn't funny, but I laughed. I wasn't laughing at being called a dago. That didn't make me mad. So far as I was concerned, a dago was just another name for an Italian. And I certainly wasn't ashamed of being an Italian. When somebody says Italian to me, I think about Rome and Venice and Michelangelo, and maybe even Italian food, none of which was embarrassing. I was laughing because I had been half afraid, for some stupid reason, that the guy Keith had thrown into the chairs had made some crack like the crack Mr. Jozak had made the day Keith had punched him and gotten us kicked off the football team. And I didn't like the idea of Keith feeling he had to protect me, or my sensitive feelings, by punching people out.

"What's so funny?" Marilyn said.

"I'm guilty," I said. "I am a dago, also known as a wop, and sometimes, between us dagos, as a paisano."

"What's that mean?"

"Italian for 'countryman,' " I said.

"It doesn't bother you?"

"I don't like it," I said, "but it's not worth fighting about."

"Well, you insisted that I tell you," she said.

"What I don't like is Keith fighting what he thinks are my battles for me," I said.

"Well, it's over and done with," Marilyn said.

Members of the VFW all have keys to let themselves in the door. I wasn't a member, and I didn't have a key, so I had to push the button and wait for the bartender to come and let me in.

"Hey, Allan," he said. "How are you?"

"I'm supposed to pick up a set of crutches," I said. "Or is it a pair of crutches?"

"Upstairs," he said. "I think somebody's in the office."

We had gone into the building from the parking lot. The door opened directly into the bar. I could tell from Marilyn's face that she thought there was something strange about a bar lined with cops and firemen in uniform at nine-thirty on Sunday morning. Civilians never can seem to remember that cops and firemen work shifts around the clock. The men at the bar had just come off the midnight-to-eight shift, and like people who get off work at five in the afternoon, were having a couple of beers before going home.

"I've never been in a VFW before," she said, as we climbed the stairs to the office on the second floor.

"That makes us even," I said. "Last night was my first country club. But fear not, fair maiden, I will protect you from the lower classes."

"That's a rotten thing to say!" she flared at me.

"Sorry," I said. "My mouth runs away with me sometimes."

"What Walter said does bother you, doesn't it?" she challenged.

"Not about being Italian," I said. "But the other part of it. Who does he think he is, anyway?"

"I don't know who *he* thinks he is," Marilyn said, "but *I* think he's a jerk."

The lady in the office knew me. Pop had been quartermaster of the Post for several years, and I'd practically grown up in it. She left the office and came back in about five minutes with a brand new set of crutches, still in their protective plastic wrapping.

"Thanks," I said.

"Staying for brunch?" she asked. "It's a good one today."

"I've had breakfast, thank you," I said. The Post always has a buffet brunch on Sunday.

"They've got both eggs benedict and oyster stew," she said.

"Thanks anyway," I said.

"This may not be very ladylike," Marilyn said, "but all I had, before my parents saw the paper and went off on their errand of mercy, was a glass of milk."

"We'll stay," I said.

"Don't look so stricken," Marilyn said. "I'll pay for my own."

"No, you won't," I said.

I had some oyster stew. Marilyn had both the stew and the eggs benedict. I wondered where she put it all.

I had guessed right about Marilyn being surprised to see the men at the bar. Tactfully she asked, "Does this place go twenty-four hours a day?"

I explained to her why it did.

"Very nice," she said. "It's really another world, isn't it?"

"Yeah, I guess it is," I said.

"It looks much more interesting than mine," she said, and she smiled at me.

Then we left and drove back to Presbyterian Hospital. As we got off the elevator, Marilyn's parents were waiting to get on it.

"The doctor's in there with him now," Mrs. Withers said. "I think they're going to keep him one more day. Just to be sure."

"You coming with us, Kitten?" Mr. Withers asked.

"I think I'll stick around," Marilyn said. "Allan can drive me home."

"What about eating?" her mother asked.

"Allan fed me," Marilyn said. "Oyster stew and eggs benedict."

"Sounds delicious," her father said. "Where did you find that?"

"At the VFW," Marilyn said. That shook them up a little.

"This may not be the time and place for this, Allan," Mr. Withers said to me, "but I wanted to thank you for last night."

"I beg your pardon?"

"I understand you kept a bad situation from getting worse," he said. "Keith sometimes . . . gets out of hand."

"You're embarrassing him, Daddy," Marilyn said. "We'll see you later." She took my arm and propelled me down the corridor to Keith's room.

Keith, as I sort of expected he would be, was protesting being kept in the hospital.

"There's not even a television," he said. "What am I supposed to do, stare at that ugly picture on the wall?"

"I'll bring your portable," his mother said.

"You gave your head quite a whack," the doctor said, and then stopped when he saw Marilyn and me.

"Dr. Furman," Mrs. Stevens said, "these are Keith's friends, Allan Corelli and Marilyn Withers."

"How do you do?" he said, and turned back to Keith. "If you feel all right tomorrow, you can go home tomorrow afternoon. I'm not even sure if we could get an ambulance today."

"An ambulance? What for?" Keith asked.

"You're not going to be able to ride in a car with your leg in a cast like that," the doctor said.

"How am I supposed to go to school?" Keith asked.

"What about in the back of the station wagon?" old Big Mouth said. "We could fold down the back seat and put one of those camping cushions in the back, and then he could sort of half sit and half lie down."

"Good idea, Allan!" Mrs. Stevens said.

"That would work, of course," Dr. Furman said. "I really hadn't thought about Keith going to school. A cushion in the back of the station wagon would work. And then you'll have to do something about his pants, too."

"I beg your pardon?" Mrs. Stevens asked.

"He's not going to be able to get that cast through his pants leg," the doctor said. We all looked at Keith's leg. He was in plaster from his upper ankle to his middle.

"We could either cut off one leg," Mrs. Stevens said. "Or open the seam and sew in some extra material."

"I'll go for cutting off the leg," Marilyn cracked innocently. "That seems to be the easiest way out of the problem."

"I mean the pants leg, dear," Mrs. Stevens said.

"Thanks a lot, Goofus," Keith said.

Mrs. Stevens went to Keith and measured the size of his cast at the knee with her fingers.

"I'll tell you what," she said. "I'll have Allan drive me home. I'll open the seam on a pair of blue jeans and sew in some extra material. Then I'll bring them and your portable TV back here. While I'm gone, you can have lunch."

"Whoopee!"

"You'd better be nice, Keith," Marilyn said. "For once, you're at our mercy."

"Allan, do you know where you can get a cushion for the station wagon?" Mrs. Stevens asked.

"Today, you mean? I think there's a place in Plainfield that sells them, and that's open today."

"Would you mind? I mean, I realize what an imposition this is, and what an imposition it's going to be until Keith is well."

There seemed to be no question in anyone's mind that (a) Keith would be chauffeured around in the station wagon, and (b) that good ol' Al Corelli would be the chauffeur.

"No, ma'am," I said. "Not at all." After all, I told myself, if I had the busted leg, Keith would have done the same thing for me.

Mrs. Stevens dug in her purse and came up with a wad of money. She handed it to me. "Take this," she said. "And let me know whenever you need any more. I really appreciate this, Allan."

"Hey, when you're at the house," Keith said, "take the Polaroid and bring me a picture of the car, will you?"

"Sure," I said.

I called my father from Mrs. Stevens's house, and he told me where the Mercedes had been taken. I told him what I was up to, and from the tone of his voice I understood that he had expected that I would become Keith's male nurse. I got the feeling that even if Keith and I couldn't stand each other's sight, I would still have been given the job because Keith was, after all, Mrs. Stevens's son.

The Discount Auto Store in Plainfield had a wide selection of station-wagon cushions, and they came in all styles, solid colors, plaids, and in pink and blue with little elephants and ducks and puppies, for people who planned to carry their babies around.

I looked over at Marilyn and saw in her eyes the same delightful thought that had come into my mind.

"We'll take the pink one," I said. "The one with the winged elephant holding the umbrella in his trunk."

"I think little Keith will just *love* it!" Marilyn said.

"How old is he?" the saleswoman asked, drawing the wrong conclusion.

"Seventeen," Marilyn replied quickly.

"And large for his age," I said.

I was in a very good mood.

We went from Plainfield to the bodyshop in Newark. The yellow Mercedes was sitting inside the building, a large concrete-block affair. There wasn't much left of it. The guy driving the Ford had apparently hit him right on the left front wheel. The wheel was tipped in at the top, almost parallel to the ground. The whole front end of the car had been knocked to the right, and there was a puddle of oil and water and transmission fluid on the floor under it. The engine had been torn off its mounts and loosened from the transmission. The force of the collision had been strong enough to twist the body of the car, too. The windshield and driver's side-door window were broken. There wasn't much left of the windshield, and the side window was cracked into a thousand pieces. I pushed on it gently and it fell apart.

"He's lucky he's alive," Marilyn said.

"What I can't understand is what he said," I thought aloud.

"What do you mean?"

"You heard him," I said. "He said the first thing he knew about the accident was when he woke up in the hospital. I wonder why he didn't see the car coming? Or at least just before it hit him?" The answer came immediately to me, but for once I kept my fat mouth shut.

Marilyn felt no such restrictions.

"Maybe he was drunk," she said. "Maybe, even *probably*, he was drunk."

She looked at me, but I didn't say anything to her. Then I took four Polaroid pictures of the wreck, and then we went back to the hospital.

CHAPTER 10

And so began my career as chauffeur and male nurse to Keith Stevens. There was one other small problem about Keith and his cast and pants legs that couldn't be solved simply by cutting open the seam and adding material.

I found this out Monday afternoon when I went to the hospital to drive him home in the station wagon.

"We're ready to go," Mrs. Stevens said, "just as soon as you help him get dressed."

"Sure," I said, since I didn't have any idea what she meant. The problem was that there was no way Keith could bend to hold his pants and slip into them. We finally figured out a way, using a broom handle, for him to get undressed by himself, but as long as he was in the cast, and he was in it six weeks, I had to be there to help him put his pants on.

He had been practicing with the crutches and was already pretty good with them, but there was a hospital rule that you had to be rolled to the door in a wheelchair, and they enforced it.

Outside the hospital he got up on his crutches and, with his mother hovering anxiously over him, made his way to the station wagon. I held the back door open for him.

"You did that on purpose," he said, taking one look at the pink cushion with the elephant on it. "I'll get you for that, Al Capone."

"It was probably all they had, dear," Mrs. Stevens said.

"Oh, no it wasn't," he said. "Was it, Al?"

"Actually, no," I said. "Marilyn and I were torn between the elephant and a blue duckie."

"I thought I detected her hand in this," he said.

He sat down on the edge of the floor and then pushed himself inside. There was plenty of room in there, and if he sat up, he could see out the window.

"I'll follow you home," Mrs. Stevens said. "Drive slowly, Allan."

"Remember how fragile I am," Keith said.

We spent the rest of the afternoon learning how he was to move around with one very stiff leg. Going up and down stairs looked to me like a nearly impossible problem on crutches, but that was fairly easy to solve. He just sat down on the stairs and moved up or down by pushing himself with his hands.

The first day I gave him a sponge bath, which was not really my idea of fun. We gave that some thought, and finally decided one solution would be to wrap the cast in Saran Wrap, and then prop the cast out of the way while he took a bath in shallow water.

Mrs. Stevens made a remark about not knowing what she would do without me, and I made some modest disclaimer. But I realized that without me, Keith would really be in a fix. His mother certainly couldn't lower him into a bathtub the way I could. It was a strain for me, and I was larger than he was. Mrs. Stevens was small and slight.

We had just made our way (me walking, Keith bumping his way down the stairs) to the recreation room when the door chimes sounded.

"Mother'll get it," Keith said. "You, Nursie, can get me a cold beer from the cooler."

"Are you supposed to be drinking beer? Aren't you on some kind of medicine?"

"Just your tender, loving care," he said. "It doesn't hurt. It just itches."

"You were lucky," I said.

"I'll drink to that," he said. "Just as soon as you get me the beer."

I had no sooner handed him the beer when there were footsteps on the stairs. I turned to look, and it was Mrs. Stevens and a cop I knew by sight, but whose name I couldn't place.

"Hey, Allan," he said. "I didn't expect to see you here."

"Nice to see you," I said.

"Keith Stevens?" he asked, and Keith nodded. "I'm Sergeant Dumbrowski, from the DA's office. I've got a subpoena for you." He walked over to where Keith was half sitting up on the couch and handed him an envelope.

"What's this all about?" Keith asked.

"The People of the Sovereign State of New Jersey versus one

Thomas T. Waldron," the sergeant said. "On a charge of driving while intoxicated."

"Oh," Keith said.

"The DA ran it through the Grand Jury this morning," the sergeant said. "The trial is scheduled for next Monday."

"Oh," Keith said, again.

"One of the assistant DA's will probably be around to see you before then," the sergeant went on, "to go over your testimony with you."

"I can't tell him a thing," Keith said. "One moment I was driving up Raymond Boulevard, and the next thing I knew I was in the hospital."

"There were other witnesses," the sergeant said. "A couple of waitresses in a hamburger joint on the corner happened to be looking out the window when Waldron ran the light and ran into you. All you'll have to testify to is that it was you in the car."

"Oh," Keith said. It was the third time he'd said "oh." He obviously didn't like any of this. I wondered if this was because he knew he had been drinking, if not drunk too, and was afraid this would come out.

"Nothing to worry about," the sergeant said. "This guy, between you and me, dug his own grave."

When the sergeant left, I left with him. I hadn't been home yet, and it was getting near suppertime. Mrs. Stevens asked me to stay for supper, but I told her the family would probably want a bulletin on Keith's condition, and that I'd better go.

About half past seven, Keith called up.

"Is this the Springview Male Nurse Service?" he asked.

"What's up?"

"I'm bored," he said. "Let's go someplace."

"Like where?"

"Well, I thought I might just pay a courtesy call on the

Withers," he said. "To thank them for coming to see me in the hospital, you see. And to show them the cast." I didn't say anything, so he went on. "I figured I'd call Goofus and see if she didn't have some friend with a Florence Nightingale—or Hotlips Houlihan—complex, who might want to tend the needs of a sick man. I figured we could buy them a hamburger or something."

He had found my weak spot of course. It hadn't really required a whole lot of deep thought on his part, but he obviously had thought about it.

"Okay," I said. "I'll be there in ten minutes."

"I'll stagger out to the curb to meet you," he said, and hung up.

The Withers house was near the country club. Actually it touched the country club. When they looked out their front door, they could see one of the greens across the street. Very nice. As I followed Keith up the walkway, I realized that I had never been in a house that big before.

Mr. Withers opened the door to us. He shook my hand quickly and then walked beside Keith as Keith went into the living room and lowered himself onto a couch with a look of noble strength in the face of pain.

"Well, how do you feel, son?" Mr. Withers said.

"Fine," Keith said bravely. "Just fine. I really came to apologize for the trouble I caused at Marilyn's party."

"Oh, forget it," Mr. Withers said. "No real harm done. Just two broken chairs."

"Just two?" Keith asked.

"Keith," Mr. Withers said, "you're impossible." But he didn't seem angry.

Marilyn appeared.

"You look disgustingly healthy for someone who nearly killed himself," she said. "How do you feel?"

"As well as can be expected under the circumstances," Keith said. "Aren't you going to say hello to Al?"

"Hi, Allan," Marilyn said to me. Her father gave me a strange look, and I had the funny feeling, a sure feeling, that he either sensed something or Marilyn had said something that gave him the idea we had a thing going. It made me a little nervous, but it wasn't all that bad. "What did Apeboy have to say about the cushion?"

"He can't repeat what I said in mixed company," Keith said. "And thank you too, Goofus."

"I'm sure Helen will like it too," Marilyn said. "Helen likes pink."

"Pink with elephants is better than plain pink," I said.

"Who's Helen?" Keith asked.

"A girl," Marilyn said. "A girl who's just thrilled with the prospect of meeting the guy who demolished his mother's car so spectacularly. She's not too bright. Pretty, but not too bright. You should get along well."

Mrs. Withers had come into the room. "Why don't you just telephone her and ask her to come here? Go get her, if necessary. Keith doesn't look in shape to go riding around."

"He doesn't mind, Mother," Marilyn said. "Allan and I got him the cutest cushion."

"I really would like to get out," Keith said. "We'll go get a hamburger or something."

So we loaded Keith back in the station wagon and went and picked up Helen. Marilyn had told it like it was. Helen was pretty, but not too bright. Her parents were a little bit afraid of him, his reputation having gone before him, but he charmed them. He was good at that.

When we got back to the station wagon from Helen's house,

Helen refused to get in the back with Keith.

"What would people think if they saw the both of us on a mattress?" she asked.

I tried to keep from laughing. Marilyn didn't bother. "They'd probably think we were bringing you both home from nursery school," she said. "But you do have a point, Helen. You ride up in front with us."

"This isn't exactly what I had in mind," Keith said.

Keith's idea of a hamburger and mine were a little different. I think of hamburger joints when someone says hamburger. Keith thinks of places like Ernie's, which is on Route 167 about ten miles out of town. The hamburgers cost $2.75, and the proprietors don't pay a whole lot of attention to how old you are when you order a beer.

I was the party-pooper. They drank beer, and I drank Seven-up. I was, after all, driving somebody else's car. I wasn't afraid that I'd get drunk or anything like that. I was afraid that somebody would back into Mrs. Stevens's station wagon, and when the cops came they would smell my breath.

I didn't really mind, because I had a chance to dance with Marilyn, and that was more than enough for me. We weren't there long. Mr. Withers had said eleven o'clock when we walked out the door, and I had no intention of getting him down on me. We were there long enough to talk about the accident, which as Marilyn had said, for some reason really turned Helen on.

Marilyn said that she and I had seen the wreck, and that it was really awful. Keith said that he hadn't seen it yet but was going to have a look after school tomorrow. Helen said she would like to see it.

"Okay," Keith said. "We'll all go. We'll pick you up after school. You go to Madame Whiskers too, Helen?"

She giggled with delight at this brilliant display of wit. Miss

Beard's School for Girls was known to the local wits as Madame Whiskers.

When we left Ernie's, Helen climbed in the back with Keith.

"What are people going to think," Marilyn asked, mocking what Helen had said before, "if they see you with Keith on the mattress?"

"Nobody's going to see us, silly," Helen said. "It's dark."

We dropped Helen off first, then Marilyn, and then started home.

"Let me give a word of advice, Allan," Keith called from the back of the station wagon. "There is a good deal to be said for good-looking blonds who are, as Marilyn says, none too bright. They're a lot less trouble than the ones who think they're as smart as you are."

"Marilyn's smarter than I am," I said. "Where does that leave me?"

"What do you mean, smarter than you?"

"The pink mattress was her idea," I said.

"Isn't that odd?" Keith replied. "She told me it was your idea." He paused. "That was when I asked her what she thought about you."

I didn't say anything.

"Don't you want to know what she had to say?" Keith asked innocently.

"Okay, what?" I said.

"She said she can't see what a nice guy like you is doing running around with me," Keith said. "Sometimes I get the feeling that Goofus doesn't entirely approve of me."

"Neither do I, when you get right down to it."

"That's no way for a nurse to talk," Keith said. "Tender, loving care is supposed to be your motto."

When I went to the station wagon in the parking lot after

school the next day, Keith was already there. He was leaning against the hood and he actually had two girls on their knees in front of him. I was a little confused at first, but then I saw they had pulled his pants leg up so they could write their names on the cast.

They thought he was some kind of hero. For some reason this bothered me.

We drove over to Miss Beard's and picked up Marilyn and Helen, and then drove to the bodyshop where the wrecked Mercedes had been towed.

A man, who looked to me somewhat like a cop, was already there. He had a camera slung from his shoulder, and he had a clipboard with some kind of a form on it, and he was writing on it when we walked up.

"Oh, Keith!" Helen gushed. "You're lucky you're alive!"

"You're Keith Stevens?" the man said, turning to look closely at him.

"Uh huh," Keith said. He was a little shaken too, I could see, by the sight of the Mercedes.

"Not much left, is there?" the man asked.

"Not much," Keith agreed.

"How'd it happen?" the man asked.

"I don't really know," Keith said. "One moment I was driving up Raymond Boulevard and then the next thing I knew, I was coming to in the hospital."

"You didn't see him before he ran into you?"

"No," Keith said. "He really must have been moving."

"You didn't see him at all?" the man asked again.

"I told you no," Keith said. "Who are you, anyway? You the fellow from the district attorney's office?"

"No," the man said. "I'm from the insurance company."

"Oh," Keith said. "Well, what's your professional opinion?"

"That car's beyond rebuilding," he said. "What we call a 'total.'"

"I figured as much," Keith said. "Damn shame. That was a fine car."

"And a very expensive one, too," the man from the insurance company replied. He looked at Keith very carefully again, and then walked out of the garage with just a slight nod of his head. He didn't say good-bye.

A couple of minutes later, having seen all there was to see, we left also. We stopped for a hamburger at the same McDonald's I'd gone to with Pop and Mrs. Stevens the night of the accident, and then we took the girls home. It was about quarter to five when I backed into Keith's driveway. There was a government car of some kind in the driveway—I could tell by the radio antenna and the blackwall tires—and Keith saw it, too.

"I think perhaps your Daddy is paying a social call on my Mommy," he said. "Isn't that ducky?"

But it wasn't my father, it was a young attorney from the DA's office. I thought he was kind of funny. He didn't look much older than us, and he was a little guy who took himself very seriously. He introduced himself as "Mister Howell," and almost from the beginning, he called Keith "son." Since he had to look up at Keith to talk to him, this was funny, too.

"Fortunately, son," Howell said, "there were disinterested witnesses, the waitresses in the Burger Barn, who saw Mr. Waldron run the stop sign. That, plus the hard evidence of the alcohol content of his blood, which indicates that he was legally intoxicated, is going to make my job easier. But I like to cover all the bases, so to speak. Tell me, son, have you ever had any moving traffic violations?"

"Yes," Keith said.

"What were they?"

"I was arrested for speeding a couple of times," Keith said. "And once for reckless driving."

"I was afraid of something like that," Howell said.

"What's that got to do with this?"

Howell didn't answer him. He asked, instead, another question.

"Tell me about the speeding violations. Did you go to court?"

"No, I forfeited the bond," Keith said.

"Where were you arrested?"

"In Massachusetts," Keith said. "It happened while I was at school."

"I see. Well, perhaps his counsel won't look that far," Howell said.

"I asked before, what's that got to do with this?"

"It might tend to discredit you as a witness, son," Howell said. "Tell me about the reckless driving charge."

"I pleaded guilty to that," Keith said.

"Also in Massachusetts?"

"No. That was in New Hampshire. I was arrested coming home from a football game."

"And this case did get to court?"

"I pleaded guilty," Keith replied.

"Anything in this state? Is your driving record clear with the Department of Motor Vehicles?"

"Not so much as a parking ticket," Keith replied.

"Well, let's go over what happened earlier that night," Howell said.

"I went to a party at the country club," Keith said. "With Allan, here."

"You're Larry Corelli's brother?" he asked.

"Uh huh," I said.

"And then what?" Howell went on.

"Allan brought me home. And I was hungry, so I went out for something to eat. I was on my way home when the accident happened."

"Where did you go to eat?"

"A place called the Peking Palace," Keith said.

"Where?"

"On Mott Street, in Newark."

"Wasn't that a long way to go?"

"I wanted Chinese," Keith said. "What's the difference?"

"I'm trying to think of the questions Mr. Waldron's lawyer is liable to ask," Howell said. "So you went to the Peking Palace and got something to eat. Did you have anything to drink?"

"I don't know how to answer that question," Keith said. "I'm seventeen. The law says eighteen."

"Let me put it this way, son. Were you intoxicated?"

"Look, the other guy ran into me!" Keith said. "Why am I getting grilled like this?"

"Were you drunk?" Howell repeated.

"No, of course not."

"But you had been drinking?"

"Off the record, I had a beer, all right? I had a beer and chop suey."

"They didn't take a blood sample, did they?"

"No," Keith replied. "I keep telling you, I was the victim, not the guy who caused the accident."

"And you said you didn't see Mr. Waldron's car at all before the impact. Is that correct?"

"That's right."

"How fast were you going?"

"Whatever the speed limit is there, that's how fast I was going," Keith said.

It went on like that for another half an hour. I thought I understood what the assistant DA was up to, but Keith didn't. I knew him well enough by then to know that resentment was growing. And I thought that he was lucky they hadn't taken a blood sample to see how much alcohol he had in his blood. He'd had plenty to drink at Marilyn's party, and Paul had called the Peking Palace a beer joint. It was very unlikely that Keith had only had one beer there. He had gone there to drink beer, not eat Chinese, as he said.

Finally Howell was satisfied, and he left telling Keith when the trial was and that he would confirm it the day before the trial with a telephone call.

CHAPTER 11

I got to go to the trial, which started on the Wednesday before Larry and Barbara got married. I got to go because I was still playing nurse and chauffeur to Keith, and I suspect that Mrs. Stevens asked my father if I could go with them. All I really knew was that my father told me I was going to do it, and that he'd squared things at school.

"They didn't like it much," he said. "But they told me that unless you suddenly change your ways, you're going to wind up in the honor society. How you're managing that and your social life is beyond me. But never kick a sleeping dog, as I always say."

That was a crack about how much I'd been going out at night. Despite all his remarks about Helen not being too bright, Keith was seeing her just about every night, and that meant I had to go along to drive the wagon. It also meant that I got to see Marilyn just as often as he saw Helen, which made it very easy to take.

I actually had more time to study, despite our just-about-every-night dates, than I could remember having before. The answer, of course, was that I wasn't playing football. When I had study halls, I was at the books instead of thinking about football. I missed football a little, I suppose, but not as much as I had at first thought I would. Another of the things I liked about Marilyn was that she wasn't a football freak. Maybe she would have been, had she been in Stockton, but she was in Madame Whiskers, where there was no football team. Some of the girls at Madame Whiskers were fans of the football team at Newark Prep, but Marilyn hadn't been bitten by that bug.

Just as soon as Apeboy, as she called Keith, was out of the cast, she was going to teach me how to play tennis. All things considered, playing tennis with Marilyn seemed a far better way to be athletic than having the cleats of some linebacker walking on your face.

And to tell the truth, for the first time I was trying to get good grades. Before, the only thing I'd really cared about was maintaining the B— average you had to have to play ball. That hadn't been much of a problem, and I hadn't had to work at it. But for some reason, maybe Marilyn, maybe because of Larry getting married and passing the lieutenant's exam, or maybe because I was just getting older, I was thinking about the future. Specifically I was thinking about college and seeing if I could get to be a lawyer. I suppose I still thought I'd be a cop, but cops with law degrees are two jumps ahead of other cops when it comes to getting promoted. And, just maybe, I thought I might be a lawyer without being a cop.

In any event I was trying to get out of high school with good grades and maybe as a member of the honor society. But even so I wondered why my father had gone to the trouble to "square things" with Richard Stockton High School. It looked to me as though all he would really have to do would be write an excuse for me to take to school on Thursday. I asked him.

"That trial won't be over in a day," he said. "Waldron's fighting it."

"What do you mean, fighting it?" I was surprised. "They've got him cold, don't they?"

"Even if Keith doesn't sue for pain and suffering," Pop said slowly, "Waldron's insurance company has to ante up an awful lot of money for that totaled Mercedes."

"Yeah, but they have the blood sample and the witnesses."

"They're already paying their lawyers," Pop said. "If they can get Waldron off, they're way ahead. If they can't get him off, what have they lost?"

"That doesn't seem fair," I said, without thinking.

"Welcome to the cold, cruel world, Allan," my father said. "Justice doesn't always triumph."

That was surprise one.

Surprise two came in the corridor of the Essex County Court House when Mrs. Stevens, Keith, and I got off the elevator. Helen Davidson was there, all dressed up, obviously waiting for us.

"What are you doing about school, dear?" Mrs. Stevens asked.

"Using up my cuts," Helen said. "We get three days' worth a year."

Keith was shook up by Helen's appearance. On one hand anybody could see he was touched, flattered, that she had come to the trial. It was a gesture of friendship, maybe even of something more. On the other hand Keith was no fool, and I know that he must have had some idea that he wasn't going to look like the knight in shining armor on the white horse.

Howell, the lawyer from the DA's office, came bustling importantly down the marble corridor to us. It wasn't Keith against Waldron, he explained. It was the Sovereign State of New Jersey against Waldron. Keith was only a witness for the prosecution, which meant that he was led off and placed under the control of a court bailiff. The only time he would appear in the court was when he was on the witness stand.

Mrs. Stevens, Helen, and I went into the courtroom. We waited. We did a lot of waiting in the next several days. Most of that first morning was spent watching what was going on at the judge's bench, much of which we didn't understand.

Lawyers and their clients (some of them well dressed, and some of them wearing blue-denim prison clothes) took their turn walking up to the judge's bench, where they held whispered, informal conferences with the judge and with other lawyers. None of us had any idea what was going on.

Finally at quarter past eleven, the bailiff, a fat, red-faced man in his sixties wearing a policeman's uniform, called out, "Docket 23-45-107, The People Versus Thomas T. Waldron."

"Ready, Your Honor," Mr. Howell called out. I saw him, for the first time, standing up behind a wooden table at the right side of the courtroom. I hadn't even seen him come in.

"Ready, Your Honor," another man called. He was standing up behind a table on the left side of the courtroom. There were three other men at the table, all about the same age, and all dressed about the same way. One of them, certainly, was the man who had run the stop sign and clobbered Keith and the Mercedes. The other two, just as certainly, were other lawyers.

"All right," the judge called. He was a little man, bald, skinny, with thick glasses, maybe forty-five years old. "Let's get on with it."

The bailiff handed him a sheath of papers. He flipped through them, and then looked at the Waldron table. The lawyer who had spoken first and the man sitting beside him got to their feet. I realized that must be Waldron. He looked like a perfectly respectable middle-aged man. He looked like my father, or Mr. Withers, except that he wasn't as well dressed as Mr. Withers.

"Mr. Waldron," the judge said, looking at him, "you are charged with violation of the criminal code of the State of New Jersey in that, on September twenty-seventh of this year, you operated a motor vehicle while intoxicated by alcohol. How do you plead, sir?"

Mr. Waldron cleared his throat. "Not guilty, Your Honor."

"Not guilty?" the judge asked.

"Yes, sir."

"So noted," the judge said. "By consent of counsel this court will also deal with another matter. Mr. Waldron, you are charged with violation of the motor vehicle code of the State of New Jersey in that on September twenty-seventh of this year, while operating a motor vehicle, you failed to heed a stop sign, and then struck a motor vehicle being driven by one Keith Stevens. How do you plead to this charge?"

"Not guilty, Your Honor," Waldron's lawyer said.

"Mr. Waldron?" the judge asked. He wanted to hear from Waldron himself.

"Not guilty, Your Honor," Mr. Waldron said.

That surprised me, and it surprised Mrs. Stevens too, for she nudged me and stuck her lower lip out thoughtfully.

"So entered," the judge said. "Is the state ready to proceed?"

"Yes, sir," Howell said, getting to his feet.

"The defense is ready, Your Honor," the lawyer who had been

talking for Waldron said, without being asked.

What came next, and it lasted until one, when we were given an hour for lunch, and from about two-fifteen until four-thirty, was the selection of jurors.

It wasn't hard to figure out, even in the beginning, what was going on. The defense lawyers wanted poor people, or what would be called lower middle-class people, people like my family and with less money, on the jury. And it wasn't hard to figure out why, either. They would be like Mr. Waldron, and they would be sympathetic to him. Howell, on the other hand, was looking for straight people, or square people maybe, the kind of people who would like to see someone who drove drunk and ran a stop sign and almost killed somebody either locked up or heavily fined.

Waldron's lawyer asked one lady if she drank. She got white in the face, said "certainly not," and I knew even before it happened that Waldron's lawyer was going to keep her off the jury.

Over lunch Keith suggested to Helen that she take off, that there was no point in her sticking around. She acted hurt and said she would go if he really wanted her to go, so of course Keith got soft and told her to stay if she wanted to. She'd come all the way to Newark on the bus, so we drove her home, and when we got there her mother came out and invited Mrs. Stevens in for a drink.

Keith took one, a scotch and water, saying he needed it. Mrs. Davidson and Mrs. Stevens ran down a long list of people they knew together. I realized that neither of them would have been allowed on the jury if Waldron's lawyer had anything to say about it.

I wasn't surprised the next morning when I picked up Keith and his mother to have Mrs. Stevens tell me that we were also picking up Helen Davidson. When we got to Newark, I looked in the back of the station wagon and saw Helen hanging onto Keith's arm as if he was going to run away.

Jury selection had been completed before the judge had adjourned the day before, so as soon as another long line of people and their lawyers had had short conferences with the judge, Mr. Howell made his opening statement.

"Ladies and gentlemen of the jury," he said. "This is really a very simple case. The state has accused Mr. Waldron of driving his automobile while he was intoxicated by alcohol. That is, when he was drunk. That's a criminal offense. The state is also accusing Mr. Waldron of another offense, a misdemeanor. We say that he violated the motor vehicle code by failing to stop at a stop sign.

"We are going to put two witnesses on the stand, two witnesses who have no interest in this case one way or the other, who saw Mr. Waldron run the stop sign, and saw him crash into a car driven by a seventeen-year-old boy. We're going to put the police officers who investigated the accident on the stand to tell you what they saw. These officers will testify that they smelled liquor on Mr. Waldron's breath, and that they saw other signs that made them suspect that he was drunk.

"They're also going to testify that they got Mr. Waldron to agree to a blood test, that they told him they thought he was drunk, and that if he said that he wasn't, a blood test would prove it one way or the other.

"Then we're going to put into evidence the results of that blood test, which show that the alcohol content of Mr. Waldron's blood was point two zero percent, which our expert witness, a medical doctor, will testify is an indication, both medically and legally, under the laws of New Jersey, that Mr. Waldron was drunk.

"And finally, we're going to put the young man he ran into onto the stand, and he will testify that he was lawfully driving along when Mr. Waldron ran through a stop sign and into him, causing a crash that, by the grace of God, didn't kill him but demolished his automobile and put him in the hospital.

"And when we've done all that, ladies and gentlemen, I'm satisfied that you'll be able to bring in a verdict that Mr. Waldron is guilt of both offenses beyond any doubt at all. I thank you."

Howell sat down. The judge looked at Waldron's defense counsel. "Mr. Davies?"

"No opening statement, Your Honor," Waldron's lawyer said.

"Very well," the judge said, but he sounded surprised. "Are you ready to call your first witness, Mr. Howell?"

"Yes, Your Honor," Howell said. "The state calls Miss Florence Horter."

The bailiff went to a door in the wall of the courtroom and called her name again. She was a woman of about thirty, and she looked more than a little nervous. She swore to tell the truth, the whole truth, and nothing but the truth by saying "I swear" as the bailiff held a battered old Bible for her to put her hand on.

Then Mr. Howell started to question her.

"Where do you work, Miss Horter?" he asked.

"At the Qwik 'n' Ezy," she said.

"That's a restaurant?"

"More like a hamburger place," she replied.

"A quick-service food place? Hamburgers and things like that?"

"Yes, sir."

"Where is this?"

"On the corner of Second and Raymond Boulevard," she said. "In Newark."

"And were you working there on the morning of September twenty-seventh?"

"Yes, sir."

"And what, if anything, did you see happen at about two

o'clock on the morning of September twenty-seventh?" Howell asked.

"Well," she said, "things was a little slow, and Ginny and me—"

"Objection!" Mr. Waldron's lawyer said, getting to his feet.

"Just tell us what you saw," Mr. Howell said.

"Things was a little slow," she began again, "and I was looking out the window with my friend—"

"Out the window? Could you see the intersection of Second Street and Raymond Boulevard?"

"Yes, sir."

"What, if anything, did you see when you looked out the window?"

"Well, this blue Ford comes down Second Street, going like hell, excuse me—"

"Do you mean that you saw a blue Ford moving at a high, or excessive rate of speed?"

"Objection," Mr. Waldron's lawyer said. "He's leading the witness."

"Overruled," the judge said. "Answer the question."

"He was speeding," the waitress went on, "if that's what you mean."

"I see. And what, if anything else, did you see?"

"He run right through the stop sign and ran into the Mercedes," she said very firmly.

"What Mercedes is that?" Howell asked.

"A little one. A yellow coupe. It was coming up Raymond Boulevard."

"You saw the Mercedes before the crash?"

"Yes, sir."

"And you saw the Ford moving at a high rate of speed run the stop sign and run into the Mercedes?"

"Yes, sir."

"Objection again, Your Honor," Waldron's lawyer said.

"Overruled again," the judge said.

"Where did he, the Ford I mean, hit the Mercedes?"

"In the front," she said. "He run into it right at the front wheel. And knocked it off the road onto the curb. It made an awful racket."

"I'm going to show you some photographs," Mr. Howell said, picking up several eight-by-ten-inch pictures from his desk. He first handed them to Mr. Waldron's lawyer, who looked at them, nodded, and then handed them to the bailiff. He carried them up to the judge, who glanced at them quickly, nodded his head, and handed them back to the bailiff who returned them to Mr. Howell. Then Mr. Howell walked to the witness box and handed them to her one at a time.

"Are these the automobiles you've been telling us about?" he asked.

"Yes, sir," she said.

"When would you say these photographs were taken?" Mr. Howell asked.

"After the accident," she said. "After the ambulance come and took them away."

"Took whom away?"

"The guy that was driving the Ford and the kid that was in the Mercedes."

"After the collision occurred," Mr. Howell asked, "what, if anything, did you do?"

"I called the cops," she said.

"You telephoned the police? Where was the telephone?"

"Right on the wall by the door," she said.

"And what did you say to the police?"

"I told them there had been an awful accident, that some drunk had run a stop sign and run into somebody," she said.

"Objection, Your Honor," Waldron's attorney said.

"If that's what she said to the police, Your Honor—" Howell said.

"Overruled," the judge said.

"The state offers these photographs as prosecution exhibits one through four," Mr. Howell said.

"Mr. Davies?" the judge asked.

"No objection, Your Honor," Mr. Davies said.

"So ordered," the judge said. "Proceed, please."

"I have no further questions at this time, Your Honor," Mr. Howell said. "Your witness, Counselor."

Mr. Davies walked up to the witness box.

"Just a few questions, Miss Horter," he said. "How did you come to be looking out the widow at the time of the unfortunate accident?"

"Things was a little slow."

"It was two in the morning, I understand?"

"Yes, sir."

"And how long had you been working when all this took place?"

"I come on at half past seven," she said.

"You went to work at half past seven? And since it was two o'clock, that meant you had been working about six and a half hours?"

"Yes, sir," she said. "I got off shift at four."

"I imagine you work pretty hard when you do work, don't you?"

"Yes, sir. Our busy time is right after midnight."

"How is that?"

"That's when the shift at Martin's Bakery changes," she said.

"I don't quite follow you," he said.

"We're right on the corner by Martin's Bakery," she said. "They change shifts at midnight. So we get business from people going on shift, before they go on, and we get more business from people getting off. You know what I mean?"

"Yes, I do," he said. "So what you're telling us is that you were taking a little break when the unfortunate accident occurred, after having been at work for six and a half hours, and after having worked hard during the time around the shift change at Martin's Bakery?"

"Yes, sir."

"Were you tired?" he asked sympathetically.

"You better believe it," she said, and laughed.

"Tell me something else, Miss Horter," he said. "Where did you get your automotive expertise?"

"I'm sorry?"

"Where did you become qualified to judge the speed of a passing automobile?" he asked.

"I don't follow you," she said.

"What makes you qualified to testify that a car is moving at a high rate of speed, to use your own words?"

"I can tell when a car's going too fast," she said. "Anybody can."

"How fast is too fast?" he asked.

"Faster than he should have been going," she said.

"What is the speed limit on Second Street?" he asked.

"I don't know," she admitted.

"Then how can you say he was going too fast?"

"He was supposed to be stopped," she said. "There was a stop sign."

He had tried to break her up, and had failed.

"No further questions," he said. "Redirect, Counselor?"

"Just to make things perfectly clear," Mr. Howell said. "Miss Horter. You are testifying, under oath, that the blue Ford failed to stop for the stop sign. Is that correct?"

"Yes, sir."

"And that you saw the blue Ford, after running the stop sign, run into the Mercedes. Is that correct?"

"Yes, sir."

"And that while you couldn't tell exactly how fast he was going, he was, in your opinion, going very fast?"

"Yes, sir."

"One final question. Did the blue Ford appear to slow down at all before running the stop sign on Second Street and entering on Raymond Boulevard?"

"No, sir, he kept right on going," she said.

"Thank you, Miss Horter," Howell said. "That will be all."

CHAPTER 12

The next witness was the other waitress. She said just about the same thing the first one had said. Even the questions sounded the same. Mr. Davies, Waldron's lawyer, brought out that she was tired after having worked hard all night, and that she wasn't qualified as an expert in judging how fast a car is going. Howell had her testify that Mr. Waldron had run the stop sign without even slowing down.

So far as I was concerned, unless the jury thought both of the women were lying—and why should they lie?—Howell had succeeded in proving that Mr. Waldron had run the stop sign and

in making it pretty likely that he had been driving too fast when
he ran it.

Then Howell summoned to the witness stand one of the cops
who had been sent to the scene of the accident. He was a good
deal more at ease than the women had been. Testifying in court
is something policemen get used to. As soon as he was sworn in,
he took a notebook from his pocket and looked at Howell as if
he hoped Howell would get the questioning over as soon as possible.

"For the record, officer, will you identify yourself?"

He said he was First Class Patrolman Victor Guarisco of the
Seventeenth Precinct.

"And you were on duty on the morning of September twenty-
seventh?"

"Yes, sir."

"What, if anything, happened at approximately 2:05 on that
morning?" Howell asked.

"The dispatcher ordered us to proceed to the site of an auto
wreck, in response to a call from a citizen, at the corner of Raymond Boulevard and Second Street," Guarisco said.

"And what, if anything, did you find when you responded to
the call?"

"There had been a wreck involving a Ford and a Mercedes,"
Guarisco said. "The first thing we did, my partner and me, was
to render first aid to the victims. Then we requested ambulances."

"There were injuries?"

"Yes, sir. The occupant of the Mercedes—"

"Just a moment, please," Howell said. "I'd like to show you
some photographs, previously entered into evidence as prosecution exhibits one through four, and ask you if they appear familiar."

He handed the photographs to him.

"Yes, sir, they're familiar," Guarisco said. "They were taken by the police photographer after the victims had been removed to the hospital. I mean, these are pictures of the collision."

"Thank you," Howell said. "Go ahead with your story."

"Well, I detected the smell of alcohol on the breath of the driver of the Ford, Mr. Waldron."

"Is Mr. Waldron in the courtroom? And if so would you please point him out?"

Guarisco pointed to Mr. Waldron.

"Let the record show that the witness identified the defendant," Howell said. "Go ahead, please."

"So, after notifying the duty sergeant, I went to Presbyterian Hospital to give Mr. Waldron a chance to take a blood test."

"Would you explain that, please?"

"The law provides that a police officer who has reason to suspect that somebody is under the influence of alcohol and has been driving a car can request that he take a blood test."

"Is this voluntary?"

"He doesn't have to take the test," Guarisco said, "but the law provides that he will lose his driver's license for a year if he refuses."

"And Mr. Waldron agreed to give a sample of his blood?"

"Yes, sir."

"Did you see the blood removed from his vein?"

"Yes, sir."

"And where was your partner while this was going on?"

"He was at the scene of the collision, interviewing witnesses," Guarisco said.

"And then you returned to the scene?"

"Yes, sir."

"Is there a stop sign erected on Second Street at that intersection?"

"Yes, sir."

"Was that sign up that night? I mean, did you see the sign, and was it visible to drivers of automobiles coming to the intersection of Second Street and Raymond Boulevard?"

"Yes, sir."

"When you returned to the scene, did you interview witnesses to the collision?"

"Yes, sir."

"If I were to tell you, Officer Guarisco, that two witnesses have testified under oath that they witnessed the blue Ford shown in those photographs proceeding down Second Street at what they described as a high rate of speed, and then running the stop sign, and then running into the other car, would that coincide with what the witnesses you interviewed told you?"

"Objection, hearsay," Mr. Waldron's lawyer said, getting to his feet.

"Overruled," the judge said.

"Yes, sir."

"What, if anything, did you do then?"

"We prepared a citation for Mr. Waldron, charging him with running a stop sign," Guarisco said. "And another citation for driving while intoxicated."

"You didn't have the results of the blood test at that time, did you?"

"No, sir," Guarisco said. "I issued the citation on the basis of my personal opinion that he was drunk."

"And if the blood test had shown that he was legally sober?"

"I don't know what you mean?" Guarisco said.

"Would you then have invalidated the citation for DWI?"

"No, sir. I thought he was drunk. I would have testified to that in court."

"Even without the blood test?"

"Yes, sir."

"And then what happened?"

"We went back on patrol," Guarisco said.

"Thank you very much, Officer Guarisco," Howell said. "Subject to recall. I have no further questions at this time. Mr. Davies?"

Mr. Davies walked up to Guarisco.

"How long have you been a police officer, Officer Guarisco?" he asked.

"Fourteen years," Guarisco said.

"And you're still only a Patrolman First Class? Any special reason?"

"I didn't score too well on the sergeant's exam," Guarisco said, embarrassed.

"Oh, I see. But you like being a police officer?"

"Yes, I do."

"Lot of friends on the force, that sort of thing?"

"Yes, sir."

"Your Honor, where's he going?" Howell said.

"I don't know," the judge admitted. "Don't stray, Mr. Davies."

"Please bear with me a little longer, Your Honor," Davies said.

"Go ahead."

"Are you familiar with a policeman by the name of Paul Corelli?" Mr. Davies asked.

"Oh, you mean Chief Corelli?" Guarisco said. "Sure, I know him. Yes, sir."

I sat up suddenly, wondering what this was all about.

"Chief Corelli? What is he chief of?" Mr. Davies asked.

"He used to be Chief of Detectives here," Guarisco said. "Now he's Chief of Police in Springview."

"Your Honor!" Howell protested again.

"Either get to the point or change your line of questioning, Mr. Davies," the judge said.

"And do you know Detective Lieutenant Lawrence Corelli?" Mr. Davies asked.

"Yes, sir," Guarisco replied. He looked as confused as I felt by this line of questioning.

"That's all, Mr. Davies," the judge said sharply. "Please approach the bench."

Davies and Howell walked up to the judge's bench and there was a whispered conference, one that annoyed Howell. He waved his arms around and kept shaking his head. Finally they turned around and Howell sat down. Davies turned to Guarisco again.

"Tell me, Officer Guarisco, at the time that you say you smelled alcohol on the breath of Mr. Waldron, did you smell the breath of the other party involved, Keith Stevens?"

"No, sir."

"Why not?" Davies asked simply.

"He was pretty badly injured," Guarisco said. "I thought his leg was broken, and he was bleeding pretty badly."

"Then you were close to him?"

"Yes."

"Close enough to smell his breath, if you wanted to?"

"If the kid had been drinking, I would have smelled it," Guarisco said.

"No further questions at this time," Davies said. "Redirect, Mr. Howell?"

"Just one question," Howell said. "If you had smelled alcohol on the breath of Keith Stevens, Officer Guarisco, would you have begun the same blood test procedures you began with Mr. Waldron?"

"Yes, sir," Guarisco said firmly.

"Thank you," Howell said. "That will be all."

The other cop was called to testify next. Under Howell's questioning he said about the same thing as Guarisco had said: that they had been dispatched to the scene of the wreck, had called ambulances, that he had smelled liquor on Mr. Waldron's breath, and that the waitresses who had been witnesses told him they had seen Waldron driving fast, running the stop sign, and crashing into Keith's car.

He even asked some of Davies's questions for him.

"Did you detect the odor of alcohol on the breath of the victim, Keith Stevens?"

"No, sir."

"Were you close enough to smell his breath?" Howell asked

"Yes, sir," he said. "Several times. First, when we first got there, and then when I helped the ambulance guys get him out of the car."

"And in your professional opinion of a police officer, there was no indication that he had been drinking?"

"No, sir."

"How long have you been on the police force?"

"Nine years."

"Do you happen to know the name of the chief of the Traffic Division?"

"Yes, sir."

"How about the name of the Juvenile Division?"

"Yes, sir."

"Would you say, in fact, that you know the names of, and are acquainted with most of the senior officers of the police department?"

"Yes, sir."

"That'll be all, thank you," Howell said. "Your witness, Counselor."

"Just one question, officer," Davies said, "before I let you go, subject to recall. My opponent left the former Chief of Detectives, Paul Corelli, off his list of senior police officers. Do you know Chief Corelli? And if so, how well?"

"I know him very well," the cop said. "He was my precinct captain for a year or so before he took over the Detective Bureau."

"You know him very well? Thank you. That's all."

"The state calls Dr. Edwin J. Sauer," Howell said, and the bailiff went to get Dr. Sauer from the witness room. He was a young man but already getting bald. His suit was a little mussed, and his glasses kept slipping down his nose as he swore to tell the truth, the whole truth, and nothing but the truth.

"Doctor," Howell said. "You are, for the record, Dr. Edwin J. Sauer, a member of the staff of Presbyterian Hospital of Newark?"

"Yes, sir."

"You are a medical doctor, licensed to practice in the state of New Jersey?"

"Yes, sir."

"Have you any other degrees, Doctor?"

"I have a PhD in analytical chemistry," he said.

"You are, in other words, fully qualified to conduct blood tests to determine the percentage of alcohol such blood might contain?"

"Yes, sir," he said. "I'm certified to conduct such tests."

"Doctor, we would all be grateful, I'm sure, if you would, in simple layman's language, tell us something about those tests."

"All right," Dr. Sauer said. "The kind of alcohol we're talking about is an organic chemical compound containing oxygen. It's commonly called grain alcohol because it's manufactured by fermenting some sort of grain. There's alcohol in beer, wine, and whiskey. In beer and wine, the law requires that the percentage of alcohol, generally somewhere from 3.5 percent to twelve or fourteen percent, be listed on the label. For whiskey, gin, brandy, that sort of thing, the term *proof* is used, and the proof must be listed on the label. One-hundred-proof whiskey is fifty percent alcohol.

"When alcohol is taken into the body, the body quickly absorbs it through the gastrointestinal track—that is, through the stomach and the intestines—into the bloodstream. This takes place relatively quickly, as I said, and the body immediately goes to work to get rid of it. Getting rid of it is harder than absorbing it. As a general rule of thumb it is possible to detect alcohol in the bloodstream up to eighteen hours after it enters it."

"Excuse me, Doctor, let me see if we've got that straight. Up to eighteen hours after someone has taken a drink, there's still alcohol in his blood?"

"Yes. Less and less as time passes, of course. But there's some left for as long as eighteen hours."

"You're not saying that someone would stay drunk for eighteen hours?"

"Oh, no. Drunkenness, intoxication, is a function of how *much* alcohol is in the blood."

"Would you explain that, please, in simple terms?"

"Well, the fuel, so to speak, which powers the brain is blood. We've learned that if there is alcohol in the blood, when the blood reaches the brain the alcohol interferes with the functioning of the brain and causes the condition we call 'drunkenness.' "

"How much alcohol are we talking about?" Howell asked.

"Tests have shown that in people not very used to drinking, there is impairment of mental ability and loss of muscular coordination with as little as one half of one tenth of a percent—zero point zero five percent—of alcohol in the blood. People who drink a good deal acquire a tolerance for alcohol, so they don't normally act drunk until there is one tenth of one percent in their blood."

"Can you tell us how this impairment was determined?"

"By laboratory testing. At many universities and medical facilities both here and abroad. People were given simple tasks to perform, and then given alcohol and asked to repeat the tests. It's relatively easy to detect impairment of ability."

"Fascinating, Doctor," Howell said. "Please go on."

"There is about as much grain alcohol in one twelve-ounce bottle of beer as there is in one ounce of whiskey, at one-hundred proof. In other words most beer contains from 4.2 percent of alcohol. Since there are twelve ounces in a standard bottle or can of beer, that means a bottle contains almost exactly one-half ounce of pure grain alcohol. Similarly one ounce of whiskey at one-hundred proof contains exactly one-half ounce of alcohol.

"Now not all of the alcohol entering the body goes into the bloodstream, but about ninety percent of it does. The other ten percent leaves the body by breathing, or in other ways.

"So tests have shown that if someone takes into the body the alcohol contained in one ounce of whiskey, or in one bottle of beer, the alcohol content of his blood will reach about point zero two five percent. In an adult the effects of that much alcohol will be very hard to detect. We can find the alcohol in the bloodstream, but as a general rule of thumb, there is no visible loss of mental ability or muscular control."

"What about one ounce of alcohol? Two bottles of beer or two drinks of whiskey?" Howell asked.

"That will raise the blood alcohol to point zero five percent," Dr. Sauer said.

"And would the person be drunk?"

"No. Not unless he or she was very sensitive to the effects of alcohol on the brain."

"Three? Three drinks of whiskey? Or three bottles of beer?"

"Now we're into the questionable area," Dr. Sauer said. "Some people would show no effects at all, particularly those who drink a good deal. Others would, at this level of blood alcohol, we're talking about point zero seven five percent with an ounce and a half of alcohol, begin to show signs of being drunk, or actually become intoxicated. It depends on the individual."

"I see," Howell said. "What about four bottles of beer? Or four drinks of whiskey?"

"That would produce a blood alcohol of one tenth of a percent. Almost without exception there would be some signs of intoxication. Now I don't mean that the individual would be falling down drunk, but his vision, judgment, muscular coordination, and so on would be obviously affected. He might talk a little loudly and feel exhilarated, that sort of thing."

"All right, Doctor. How about five bottles of beer? Or five drinks? What can you tell us, as a medical expert, of the effect of that much alcohol on the body?"

"Five drinks or five beers would be two point five ounces of alcohol. That would raise the alcohol in the blood to point one two five percent. Many authorities feel that this constitutes legal intoxication. There would be clear signs of mental and muscular impairment."

"Many authorities, but not all. Is there a point, Doctor, at which all, or substantially all, medical authorities are in agreement that so much alcohol in the bloodstream would indicate the individual was drunk?"

"I think so," Dr. Sauer said. "Most experts in the field agree that a blood test showing the presence of zero point one five alcohol is clear proof that the individual has lost so much control of his mental and muscular processes that he or she must be deemed intoxicated."

"How much was that again?"

"Zero point one five percent. Fifteen parts in one thousand."

"Using the bottles of beer and one-ounce drinks of whiskey, we've been using so far, how many beers, or drinks of whiskey, would this equal?"

"Six beers or six drinks."

"Six beers or six drinks?"

"That is correct, sir."

"You said before that the body immediately tries to get rid of alcohol, but that it's a slow process. Did I understand that correctly?"

"Yes, sir."

"Can you tell us, in layman's terms, how fast?"

"The liver will eliminate, by oxidation, about one ounce of alcohol per hour. That's a rule of thumb, of course. As I said before, some stays in the blood for as long as eighteen hours."

"Let me put the question to you this way, Doctor, just so that the ladies and gentlemen of the jury understand everything as well as they can. If I took one drink at twelve o'clock, and then another at one o'clock, and another at two o'clock, and so on from noon to midnight, would I be very drunk?"

"You probably wouldn't be drunk at all," Dr. Sauer replied. "Your liver would be oxidizing the liquor as fast, or faster, than you were taking it in. There would be traces in your blood, but you wouldn't suffer any noticeable impairment."

"What if I took two drinks every hour on the hour?"

"Just about the same thing. Your liver could handle that."

"Now, what if I took two drinks on the half hour?"

"What do you mean?"

"Would I get drunk, and how soon?"

"Hypothetically, you mean?"

"Yes, please. Hypothetically."

"Let's say you started to drink at noon," Dr. Sauer said, "and had two drinks to start off. That would place one ounce, roughly, of alcohol in your blood, raising the count to point zero five percent. There would be no visible signs of intoxication. In thirty minutes the liver would oxidize half of that alcohol, lowering the alcohol count to point zero two five percent. Drinking two more drinks would raise it to point zero seven two five percent. That much alcohol in the bloodstream would be regarded as questionable."

"I don't quite follow you."

"It would make some people drunk, but others would not be. Those with a high tolerance to alcohol would probably be unaffected."

"Some people, in other words, can take two drinks at noon, and then two drinks thirty minutes later, and still be sober?"

"That is correct."

"Well, what about someone taking two drinks at noon, two more drinks at 12:30, and then two more at 1:00 o'clock?"

"That would be a total of six drinks, or three ounces of alcohol. But the liver, during that hour would oxidize one ounce of alcohol, which would mean there would be two ounces in the bloodstream. That would represent point one zero percent."

"Would that be proof of intoxication?"

"Not absolutely. Nine times out of ten an individual with that high a percentage of alcohol in his blood would exhibit loss of mental and/or muscular control."

"Nine times out of ten someone who has had six drinks in an hour and a half would, in layman's terms, be at least a little drunk?"

"Yes, sir, that's correct."

"What about taking another two drinks in the next thirty minutes, I mean a total of eight drinks in two hours?"

"That would be a total of four ounces of alcohol, less 1.5 ounces which the body would have gotten rid of. That would result in a blood alcohol count of about point one five percent. The individual would be drunk."

"All authorities would agree on that?"

"Yes, sir, I'm sure they would. There would be unmistakable mental and physical impairment at that level."

"Eight drinks in two hours would, beyond any reasonable doubt, make anyone drunk?"

"Yes, sir."

"Even someone with a high tolerance for alcohol?"

"Yes, sir."

"Doctor, on the morning of September twenty-seventh, were you on duty at the Presbyterian Hospital?"

"Yes, sir."

"And on the morning of September twenty-seventh, did you have occasion to draw blood from a man brought to the hospital by ambulance, and accompanied by the police, and if so, is that man in this courtroom?"

"Yes, sir. Mr. Waldron."

"Would you point him out to us, please?"

Dr. Sauer pointed at Mr. Waldron.

"Let the record show the witness identified the defendant," Howell said. "And after you drew a sample of Mr. Waldron's blood, Doctor, did you, using standard and accepted medical laboratory techniques, determine the percentage of alcohol in that blood?"

"Yes, sir."

"And what was the percentage of alcohol, Doctor, that your laboratory tests proved to be in Mr. Waldron's blood?"

"My tests indicated that there was in Mr. Waldron's blood approximately point two one five percent of alcohol," Dr. Sauer said.

"How much?"

"Point two one five percent," Dr. Sauer said.

"In your professional, expert opinion, Doctor," Howell asked, "would that indicate that he was intoxicated by reason of excessive intake of alcohol?"

"Yes, it would."

"Slightly drunk, or very drunk?"

"Very drunk."

"Can you think of any other expert in the field of medicine who would disagree with that judgment, Doctor?"

"No, sir, I cannot."

"Thank you very much, Doctor," Howell said. "Your witness, Mr. Davies."

"Your Honor," Mr. Davies said, "may I respectfully draw your attention to the hour, and offer the suggestion, with the consent of my colleague, Mr. Howell, of course, that the interests of justice might better be served if I began my cross-examination of Dr. Sauer after lunch?"

"Any objection, Mr. Howell?" the judge asked.

"None, Your Honor," Howell replied, standing up.

"We'll adjourn for lunch, then," the judge said, "until one-fifteen."

When Helen, Mrs. Stevens, and I went to the witness room to

collect Keith, a policeman told us that he would be fed with the other witnesses who were yet to testify, and he couldn't eat with us. I wound up having lunch with Keith's mother and Helen, who I had already come to think of as Keith's girl.

"I don't really see why that man doesn't plead guilty and get it over with," Mrs. Stevens said. "What chance does he have? I mean, two witnesses saw him run the stop sign, and then the doctor testified that he was legally, medically drunk. What can he hope to accomplish?"

"He hopes to get off, that's what he hopes to accomplish," I said.

"Don't be absurd!" she said, and she used that tone of voice adults use sometimes and which I knew meant that anything I said would not be listened to. She had made up her mind.

I thought I had it figured out, or at least had a good idea of what Davies was going to do, and when we went back in court I found out that I was right. It didn't make me feel good.

"Dr. Sauer," Davies began, "I found your explanation of blood alcohol very interesting, as I'm sure the ladies and gentlemen of the jury did. Tell me, Doctor, how many such blood tests do you administer in the course of say, thirty days? How many a month?"

Sauer looked thoughtful. "Depends. Somewhere between twenty and twenty-five or thirty, I suppose."

"An average of one a day? Or nearly that many?"

"I suppose," Dr. Sauer said. "As an average. On weekends I might conduct four or five in one night, and then there are periods when I conduct none at all for three to five days."

"But as an average, one a day, approximately?"

"Yes, sir."

"Who pays for these tests, Doctor?" Davies ased.

"I beg your pardon?"

"Did Mr. Waldron pay for his blood test? Or did you send him a bill, or plan to?"

"No, sir," Sauer said. "The city pays for the bill. Or the county. Or the state. It depends on who asks for the test."

"Oh, I see. If a city policeman wants to have someone's blood tested to see if he's drunk, the city pays for the bill?"

"Yes, sir."

"And if it's a county law-enforcement officer, say a park policeman or a deputy sheriff, then the county would pay?"

"That's correct."

"And if a highway patrolman, or another state law-enforcement officer asks for the test, the state pays your fee?"

"That's right."

"And what is your fee, Doctor?"

"What's this got to do with anything?" Howell asked, getting to his feet.

"I think its germane, Your Honor," Davies said.

"Go ahead, Doctor," the judge said. "Answer the question."

"Twenty-five dollars," Dr. Sauer said.

"You charge twenty-five dollars. And what exactly do you do for that twenty-five dollars, Doctor?"

"I either draw a blood sample myself or supervise a nurse in drawing the blood, and then I conduct the laboratory analysis," Dr. Sauer said.

"Let's talk about that," Davies said. "Is that a very complicated laboratory procedure?"

"No, it's not," Dr. Sauer said.

"A test to determine the percentage of alcohol in blood can, in fact, be accomplished by someone who is not a doctor of medicine, isn't that right?"

"Yes, sir."

"It is, in fact, a relatively simple procedure?"

"Yes, it is."

"But you still charge—and the city, county, and state governments still pay—twenty-five dollars each time you conduct such a test at their request?"

Dr. Sauer looked either angry or embarrassed. Probably both I thought.

"That's correct." he said.

"You testified you conduct from twenty to thirty such tests a month," Davies said. "Let's take the lower figure. Twenty tests at twenty-five dollars each amounts to $500 a month, doesn't it, Doctor? Thirty tests would mean $750 a month. It would then seem to be a fair statement that the government pays you between $500 and $750 a month to serve as their expert in whether or not someone has had too much to drink, doesn't it, Doctor?"

"You could put it that way, I suppose," Dr. Sauer said.

"Tell me this, Doctor. As a rough rule of thumb, of say every ten blood-alcohol tests that you administer, how many of those tested have, in your professional judgment, a blood-alcohol content which indicates to you that they are, in fact, intoxicated?"

"Out of ten tests, all ten. I kept a set of figures for a while, for my own information. I found that one in twenty-five people sent to me for such an examination by the police were not, to judge by their blood-alcohol content, drunk."

"One in twenty-five were not?"

"That's correct."

"Phrased another way that's the same thing as saying that ninety-six percent of the people sent to you by the police to see if they are drunk turn out to be, in your professional opinion, guilty as charged?"

"Objection, Your Honor!" Howell said.

"I'll rephrase," Davies said. "Let me put it to you this way, Doctor: any of the various law-enforcement officers who have some experience in this area over a period of say, a year, and were familiar with your operation at the hospital, could send someone

to you, and the chances are ninety-six out of a hundred that you
would find that he was drunk, isn't that so?"

"Objection!" Howell said.

"Sustained."

"I withdraw the question," Davies said. "Redirect, Mr. Howell?"

"Please," Howell said. "Dr. Sauer, I'm really sorry to have to get
into your professional life this way, but the question has been
raised. What is your primary medical function at Presbyterian
Hospital?"

"I'm an anesthesiologist," Dr. Sauer said.

"By that you mean you specialize in placing people, as we
laymen think of it, to sleep, so they will not experience pain
during surgery?"

"Correct."

"And you assist women, as an anesthesiologist, in childbirth?"

"I'm on call to render whatever medical services are required
of me," Dr. Sauer said.

"And does the practice of your primary medical specialty,
Doctor, require that you have a greater knowledge of human
blood than say, a general practitioner?"

"I would suppose so, yes, if you wanted to put it that way."

"Doesn't the practice of anesthesiology involve the introduction
into the blood system of certain chemical substances which render the patient unconscious?"

"Yes, sir."

"And while the patient is asleep, your function is to constantly
monitor the condition of his blood?"

"Yes, sir. That and any other signs."

"How often do you function as an anesthesiologist, Doctor? I
mean how many times a week, or a month, do you assist surgeons
and others with your skills?"

"On the average of two times a day."

"And you charge for this service?"

"If the patient is able to pay, or has insurance, yes."

"Then you don't charge all the time?"

"Presbyterian has both an active emergency service and a substantial charity operation," Dr. Sauer said. "I kept track of that, too. I am generally able to charge for my services, or to collect my fee, in one case out of three."

"Of all the time you spend, professionally, in the hospital, Doctor, how much of it is spent administering blood tests to determine the percentage of alcohol?"

"A very small percentage."

"Can you tell us how small?"

"Less than ten percent. Less than five percent. A very small percentage."

"And are there other doctors who conduct the same sort of tests for the government when asked?"

"Oh, there's three or four of us that do," Dr. Sauer said.

"Let me see if I can put that all together, Doctor. You are primarily an anesthesiologist, who spends no more than five percent of your time conducting blood-alcohol tests."

"That is correct."

"Can you offer an opinion as to why the police, from time to time, request that you do conduct such tests?"

"They don't request that *I* conduct them," Dr. Sauer said. "They request that the hospital conduct them. Whichever physician is qualified to make such examinations and who is available, conducts them."

"And can you offer an opinion why it is that so high a percentage—I believe you said ninety-six percent—of those sent to you for a blood-alcohol test are found to have, in fact, a percentage of blood alcohol proving them drunk?"

"Very probably because the police send only those people to us they feel are drunk."

"Why would they do that?"

"To have medical evidence supporting their observations."

"Thank you again, Doctor," Howell said. "That's all I have to ask you right now." He turned to the judge. "The prosecution rests, Your Honor."

Mrs. Stevens turned to me, shocked. "He's forgotten Keith!"

"Your Honor," Mr. Davies said. "The list of witnesses I was given, listing the witnesses the prosecution intended to call, included the alleged victim of this unfortunate accident, one Keith Stevens."

"The prosecution rests, Your Honor," Howell repeated.

"In that case, Your Honor, the defense wishes to state its intention to call Keith Stevens as a hostile witness. Is he available to testify?"

"Yes, he's available," Howell said.

"All right, Mr. Davies," the judge said. "Are you ready to proceed?"

"The defense calls Keith Stevens," Mr. Davies said.

The bailiff called Keith's name at the door to the witness room, and a moment later Keith swung through it on his crutches. He moved so quickly that I wondered if he was trying to show off how well he could manage them.

He got in the witness box, and the judge told him he could sit down while he swore to tell the truth on the bailiff's Bible.

Then Mr. Davies walked up to him.

"You are Keith Stevens?" Mr. Davies asked.

"Yes, sir."

"Where do you live, Keith?" Davies asked.

"In Springview," Keith said, and added his exact address.

"And your occupation?"

"Student," Keith replied.

"Where?"

"At Richard Stockton High School in Springview."

"What year?"

"I'm a senior."

"How old are you?"

"Seventeen."

"You're a very large young man," Mr. Davies said. "Ever play any football?"

"Yes, sir."

"For Stockton High?"

"No, sir."

"Where, then?"

"Saint Matthew's School," Keith said.

"Where is that?"

"In Massachusetts," Keith said.

"You played at Saint Matthew's School, but you're not playing for Stockton? Why is that?"

"I guess you could say I didn't make the team," Keith said. I winced, knowing what was coming.

"Is that so?" Mr. Davies said thickly sarcastic. "Would that possibly be because you had a disagreement with one of the coaches?"

"Yes," Keith said.

"A disagreement during which you punched the coach in the mouth with your fist?"

"Yes," Keith said very faintly.

"And a disagreement which resulted in a brawl, and a disagreement which saw not only you, but your best friend, thrown off the football team as brawlers?"

"Your Honor, we're not discussing a football team here," Mr. Howell said.

"We are trying to find out just what sort of a witness we have," Mr. Davies replied.

"If that was an objection, Mr. Howell," the judge said, "it's overruled. Go ahead, Mr. Davies."

"I'll ask you again, Keith," Mr. Davies said. "Did this little disagreement you're talking about end up in a brawl, a brawl which saw both you and your best friend kicked off the team?"

"I'm not sure if we got kicked off or quit," Keith said.

"But it did end up in a brawl?"

"They ganged up on me," Keith said. "Al came to my help."

"Al? Would that be Allan Corelli?"

"Yes," Keith said.

"Whose father was formerly Chief of Detectives in Newark, and is now Chief of Police in Springview?"

"That's right."

"Well, let's go on to something else, Keith," Mr. Davies said. "How long have you been driving?"

"A couple of years," Keith said.

"But I though you said you were seventeen."

"I am."

"You can't get a driver's license in New Jersey until you're seventeen. Do you mean to say that you have been driving less than a year? Or that you have been driving several years, some of it without a license?"

Keith looked a little confused, and didn't answer him immediately.

"Don't bother to answer," Mr. Davies said. "It's not important."

"I have known how to drive for several years," Keith said. "I got my license when I turned seventeen."

"Well, why don't you tell us about this accident?" Mr. Davies said. "What kind of a car were you driving?"

"A Mercedes," Keith said.

"What kind of a Mercedes?"

"A coupe," Keith said.

"An older model?"

"Last year's model," Keith said.

"Pretty nice car is it?"

"It was a beautiful car," Keith said.

"Fast, I'll bet," Mr. Davies said. "What is the top speed of a car like that?"

"A hundred twenty, I suppose, something like that."

"You ever drive it that fast?" Mr. Davies asked.

"No, sir."

"But you have driven it fast, haven't you?"

"Yes, I have," Keith said.

"Faster than the speed limit? And remember you're under oath before you answer that question."

"Yes, sir, I've driven it over the speed limit," Keith said.

"Do you have any idea how much money a car like that costs?"

"I don't know," Keith said. "Fifteen, sixteen thousand."

"Would you be surprised if I told you that a professional automobile appraiser felt that the car you were driving, before you wrecked it, of course—"

"Objection!" Howell said.

"A matter of semantics," Mr. Davies said. "I'll rephrase. Before *it was* wrecked. The question now is would you be surprised if I told you that a professional auto appraiser feels that the car you were driving, before it was wrecked, was worth $18,500 to $19,000?"

"No, sir, I wouldn't be surprised."

"Was it your car, Keith?"

"It belongs to my mother," Keith said.

"And what does your mother drive, when you're off driving this $19,000 car?"

"She has another car."

"In point of fact, Keith," Mr. Davies said, "she has two other cars, doesn't she? A Ford station wagon, and another Mercedes."

"That's right."

"The other Mercedes is a sedan, isn't it? A 280 SE?"

"Yes."

"Would you say it was worth more or less than the coupe?"

"I don't know."

"Or about the same thing?"

"I told you, I don't know. I didn't buy either one of them."

"Would you be surprised to hear a figure of $21,500 for the sedan?"

"No, I wouldn't be surprised."

"Well, let's get to the accident. The accident occurred in the early morning hours of the twenty-seventh of September. I'm interested in how you spent the evening of the twenty-sixth of September."

"I went to a party," Keith said.

"Where was the party?"

"At the Raven's Rock Country Club," Keith said.

"Are you a member of Raven's Rock?"

"I'm a junior member. My mother is a member."

"I see. So you gave a party at Raven's Rock Country Club."

"No. I went to a party, I was a guest," Keith said.

"I see. And did you go alone?"

"No, I didn't"

"With whom did you go?"

"With Allan Corelli."

"Chief Corelli's son? The one who had been in the brawl which saw you thrown off the Stockton football team? That Allan Corelli?"

"That's right."

"And which of the two Mercedes, or perhaps the Ford station wagon, did you drive?"

"We went in Allan's father's car," Keith said.

"Allan Corelli, the Chief's son, borrowed his father's car?"

"Yes, sir."

"His father's personal car, not his father's official police car, I presume."

"His father's personal car," Keith said.

"I mean it didn't have a police radio, or a flashing light, or a siren, did it?"

Keith got red in the face.

"Answer the question, please," Davies said.

"It has both a radio and bubble-gum machine," Keith said.

"A bubble-gum machine? A *bubble-gum* machine?"

"That's what you call the flashing light thing," Keith said. "The one in Mr. Corelli's car comes off. It was off when we were in the car."

"I see," Mr. Davies said. "Well, I must say I think it was very nice of Chief Corelli to let you use his car. Tell me about the party."

"It was a birthday party," Keith said.

"I see. Complete with a birthday cake?"

"Yes, sir."

"And was there anything in the way of alcoholic beverages served at this party?"

Keith glowered at him.

"I asked you a question, young man," Davies said.

"Yes, sir," Keith said.

"What alcoholic beverages were being served?" Davies pursued.

"There was some beer," Keith said. "And some champagne."

"*Champagne?* Champagne and beer? What an odd combination. Tell me, Keith, did you have any of the champagne? Or did you have any of the beer?"

"I had a couple of beers," Keith said.

"A couple of beers? Couple meaning two?"

"Yes, sir."

"Then you weren't drunk, if you had only two beers, when you got in the fight, were you?"

"I wasn't drunk," Keith said.

"But you did get in a fight, didn't you?"

"It wasn't a fight," Keith said.

"Did you or did you not throw a guest, a young man, against the wall, breaking two chairs in the process?"

"I guess I pushed him," Keith said lamely.

"Hard enough to break two chairs?"

"I guess so," Keith said.

"And then what happened?"

"I left."

"And did Chief Corelli's son go with you?"

"Yes, he did."

"Was he drunk?"

"No, he wasn't drunk," Keith said. "He wasn't drunk, and I wasn't drunk."

"Of course not," Davies said. "Do you happen to remember what time this was?"

"No, I don't."

"How about ten o'clock?" Davies asked. "Would that seem a reasonable estimate of the time?"

"I told you, I don't remember," Keith said.

"You are wearing a wristwatch, I see. You weren't wearing it that night?"

"I don't remember what time we left the country club," Keith said.

"All right, we'll let that pass. Where did you go after you left the country club?"

"Allan drove me home," Keith said. "And then he went home."

"He was still driving Chief Corelli's car?"

"Yes, he was."

"And then what did you do?"

"I realized I was hungry and went out for something to eat."

"Was anyone at home when you got there?"

"No, sir."

"Your mother was out?"

"Yes, she was."

"Do you happen to know where she was?"

"She went to dinner and the theater."

"Do you know with whom?"

"With Mr. Corelli," Keith said.

"Chief Corelli, you mean?"

"That's right."

"So you went out for something to eat. Where did you go?"

"To a Chinese place in Newark," Keith said.

"Does it have a name?"

"The Peking Palace," Keith said.

"That was some distance to go just to get something to eat, wasn't it?"

"I wanted Chinese," Keith replied.

"And did you eat Chinese, as you put it?"

"Yes, sir."

"And by any chance did you have anything to drink while you were in the Peking Palace?"

"I had a couple of beers," Keith said.

"You had a couple of beers," Mr. Davies repeated. "And then what?"

"Then I started home," Keith said. "That's when he ran into me, on the way home."

"And what time was that?"

"About two in the morning," Keith said.

"About two in the morning," Mr. Davies repeated. "How long were you in the Peking Palace having Chinese and a couple of beers?"

"A couple of hours, I suppose," Keith said.

"You suppose. Do you think it's possible that you had more than a couple of beers. Three, for example?"

"Possibly."

"Four?"

"I don't think so," Keith said.

"But it is possible?"

"I don't think so."

"You can't remember, in other words?"

"If you're implying that I was drunk, I wasn't," Keith said.

"Let's get to the accident," Mr. Davies said. "You were going north up Raymond Boulevard when the accident occurred?"

"Yes, sir."

"And Mr. Waldron was coming onto Raymond Boulevard, heading east, from Second Street?"

"I don't really know," Keith said. "I didn't see him."

"You didn't see him?" Mr. Davies asked incredulously.

"No, I didn't see him," Keith said firmly. "One moment I was riding up Raymond Boulevard, and the next thing I knew, I was in the hospital."

"You didn't see Mr. Waldron, or you didn't see his car?"

"I didn't see him or his car," Keith said.

"That's very interesting," Mr. Davies said. "It would seem to me that since the accident, as I understand it, occurred when Mr. Waldron's car collided with the left front of your car, you should have."

"Your Honor," Mr. Howell said, getting to his feet, "I'm not, and I don't think the jury is, interested in Mr. Davies's opinions."

"Is that an objection, Mr. Howell?" the judge asked.

"Yes, sir."

"Sustained. The jury will ignore Mr. Davies's last observation," the judge said. "He is not a witness in these proceedings. Please watch yourself, Mr. Davies."

"I beg the court's pardon," Davies said. "Let me see if I have this straight, Keith. You are testifying, under oath, that you did not see Mr. Waldron's car before the collision. Is that correct?"

"That's right," Keith said.

"How many beers did you say you had at the Peking Palace?"

"Objection, Your Honor," Howell said.

"On what grounds?"

"He's badgering the witness," Howell said.

"Restrain your sarcasm, Mr. Davies," the judge said.

"All right, Keith, then what? You say the next thing you knew was when you woke up in the hospital."

"Yes, sir."

"Did your mother come to visit you at the hospital that morning?"

"Yes, sir."

"And did she come alone?"

"No, sir. Mr. Corelli drove her."

"Chief Corelli, you mean?"

"Yes, sir."

"How did he get involved, do you know?"

"I guess Mother called him."

"And he came running? The good Samaritan? The family friend?"

"Yes, sir, I suppose so."

"A close family friend who was likely to have some influence if there was some problem with the law?"

"That's a cheap shot!" Keith said angrily. "He came as a friend, and it had nothing to do with the fact that he's a cop!"

"Just answer the question, please," Davies said.

"Objection, Your Honor," Howell said. "That calls for a conclusion on the part of the witness."

"Sustained," the judge said. "I'm surprised that someone of your legal experience, Mr. Davies, has to be reminded of that."

"I beg the court's pardon," Davies said. "Tell me, Keith," he said, "were you charged by the police, before or after Chief Corelli's visit to the hospital, with any offense, whatever?"

"No, I wasn't," Keith said, his voice rising.

"And they didn't test your blood, either, did they?" Mr. Davies asked.

"No, they didn't," Keith said.

"But you have had run-ins with the law involving motor vehicles, haven't you, Keith?"

"Yes, I have," Keith said.

"Not here, I mean, in Chief Corelli's jurisdiction, but elsewhere?"

"Objection, Your Honor!" Howell said.

"I'll rephrase," Davies said. "Is it true, Keith, that you have several times been charged with speeding?"

"Yes, sir."

"And isn't it also true that you pleaded guilty to a charge of reckless driving?"

"Yes, sir."

"And isn't it also true that at two o'clock on the morning of

September twenty-seventh, that you were speeding up Raymond Biulevard, recklessly speeding, in fact, when this collision occurred? And that the reason you didn't see Mr. Waldron was that you yourself were befuddled by alcohol?"

"No, damn it, it's not!" Keith said.

"Watch your language, young man!" the judge said angrily.

"I'm sorry," Keith said.

"I'm waiting," Mr. Davies said.

"For what?" Keith said.

"For your reply to my question."

"No, it isn't true. I wasn't speeding, and I wasn't drunk."

"I have no further questions of this witness," Mr. Davies said. The tone of his voice made it perfectly clear that Keith was not only a liar, but a bad one. "Your witness, Counselor," he said to Mr. Howell.

CHAPTER 14

"Just a few questions, Keith," Mr. Howell said. "First of all, were you drunk when Mr. Waldron ran into you?"

"No, sir," Keith said firmly.

"And as I understand it, you were unconscious from the moment Mr. Waldron ran into you until you woke up in the hospital?"

"Yes, sir."

"Do you remember speaking to any police officer at all that night? I mean at the scene of the accident? Or in the hospital?"

"No, sir."

"And do you know how the hospital came to call your mother?"

"No, sir."

"Can you guess?"

"Well, I have one of those cards in my wallet, you know, that say who to call in an emergency."

"Do you happen to have anything in your wallet with Chief Corelli's name on it?"

Keith thought a moment, and then said, "No, sir."

"Did you ask anyone in the hospital, anyone at all, to notify Chief Corelli that you had been in an accident?"

"No, why should I?" Keith asked.

"But you weren't surprised when he showed up at the hospital with your mother?"

"No, sir, I don't think I was."

"Was anyone with your mother besides Chief Corelli?"

"Yes, sir, Allan was."

"In other words, your friend Allan Corelli came along because he had heard you were hurt?"

"Yes, sir."

"And is this Allan Corelli, the son, doing anything now for you?"

"Yes, sir," Keith said. "He helps me get dressed, and he drives me back and forth to school. He drove me here today."

"In other words, he's your friend?"

"Yes, sir."

"Finally, Keith, did you sign a warrant charging Mr. Waldron with anything?"

"No, sir."

"In fact you have made no accusations at all in this case, have you?"

"I'm afraid I don't understand the question."

"You don't know, do you, whether or not Mr. Waldron ran a stop sign before he ran into you?"

"No, I don't now that. I heard it, but I don't know it."

"And you didn't see him that night at all, did you?"

"No, sir."

"And therefore you have no idea whether he was drunk or sober?"

"No, sir, I don't."

"I'm sure that His Honor, when he charges the jury, will remind the jury that the charges in this case have been brought by the State of New Jersey and the City of Newark. That they are accusing Mr. Waldron of violating the law, not you."

"Yes, sir," Keith said.

"No further questions," Mr. Howell said. "Redirect?"

"How many beers did you say you had at the Peking Palace?" Mr. Davies called from his table.

"Two or three," Keith said angrily.

"That's all," Mr. Davies said. "No further questions."

"Are you ready to proceed, Mr. Davies?" the judge asked.

"Yes, Your Honor," Mr. Davies said. "I am."

"Well, let's get on with it," the judge said.

"The defense calls Thomas T. Waldron," Mr. Davies said. Mr. Waldron got up from behind the table and walked to the witness box and was sworn in.

"For the record," Mr. Davies began, "you are Thomas T. Waldron of 350 Weequahic Avenue in Newark?"

"Yes, sir."

"Are you married, Mr. Waldron?"

"For twenty-three years," he said.

"Any children?"

"We have six," he said. "Four boys and two girls."

"And what is your profession, Mr. Waldron?"

"I'm a crane operator," Waldron said. "My trade is crane operator. But I'm an officer of the union. I mean, I don't actually run a crane anymore. I do union business."

"I see," Davies said. "And what were you doing on Second Street at two o'clock on the morning of September twenty-seventh?"

"I was going home," Waldron said.

"From where?"

"There was a dispute on the docks—my union represents the crane operators at Port Newark. And I'd been called down there to handle it."

"Let me see if I have that straight. There was some sort of labor-management dispute at the docks at Pork Newark, and as an official of the union, you went there to see what could be done about it?"

"Yes, sir, that's about it."

"Isn't that an odd hour to have a business discussion?" Davies asked.

"No, sir," Waldron said. "Not really. The docks operate twenty-four hours a day, seven days a week, and arguments come up all the time."

"In other words you could say that what you were doing was a perfectly natural thing for you to do?"

"Yes, sir."

"When you came to the intersection of Second Street and Raymond Boulevard, did you see a stop sign?"

"Yes, sir. It's right on the corner. You can't miss it."

"And did you stop for that stop sign?"

"Yes, sir. I stopped for it."

"And then what happened?"

"I turned onto Raymond Boulevard," he said, "up Raymond

Boulevard from downtown, if you know what I mean."

"And then?"

"Then I saw this Mercedes, a bright yellow one, coming up Raymond Boulevard going pretty fast. I turned to avoid getting hit, but I guess I didn't see him in time, or I didn't move fast enough, and we ran into each other."

"I see. You couldn't get out of his way, in other words?"

"That's the truth of it," Mr. Waldron said.

"And then what happened?"

"Well, I guess I passed out," Mr. Waldron said. "I gave my head a whack on the windshield. The next thing I know, the cops are pulling me out of my car and putting me on a stretcher. Then they put me in an ambulance and took me over to Presbyterian."

"Had you been drinking, Mr. Waldron?"

"I had two beers," he said firmly.

"Where was that?"

"At the Port of Call," he said. "That's a restaurant. By the gate to the docks. What happened is that when I got to the docks, everybody was pretty steamed up. You now what I mean, both sides were excited. So I suggested that we all go over to the Port of Call and have a cup of coffee and talk things over calm. You know what I mean? Well, we did, but instead of coffee, they wanted beer, so I had a couple with them. To go along, you know what I mean?"

"But this meeting in the Port of Call was a business meeting? I mean, it wasn't a couple of the guys stopping off for a couple of beers: you were there on business."

"That's right."

"And to do your job properly, you knew you had to be sober, didn't you?"

"Absolutely," Mr. Waldron said. "You really have to stay on your toes in a situation like that."

"I'm sure you do. So I presume that you solved the problem?"

"Yeah. We talked it out and came to an agreement."

"And then you started home, and on the way home, the collision occurred?"

"That's right."

"And you were taken to the hospital?"

"That's right."

"And what, if anything, happened at the hospital?"

"Well, I asked the cop how the other guy was. I was worried about him, of course. We really hit each other bad. And the cop said he'd hurt his leg but that he would be all right. And then he said that he would recommend I take a blood test. Or give blood for a blood test, you know what I mean. He said that would clear up any question of whether or not I had been drinking."

"Did you tell the police officer that you had, in fact, had a couple of beers?"

"Yes, I did," Waldron said. "That's why he said he would recommend that I have my blood tested. He said they could tell how much you'd had to drink."

"What you're saying then, is that you voluntarily took the test to prove, beyond any reasonable doubt, that you were sober?"

"That's it, exactly," Waldron said. "I wanted to get everything out in the open. I didn't want anybody making suggestions that I was bombed."

"By bombed, you mean intoxicated?"

"Right."

"Well, then, Mr. Waldron, what was your reaction when you were placed under arrest, charged with drunken driving, and taken to jail?"

"I didn't understand it at all," he said.

"What happened in jail?"

"Well, they threw me in a cell with some other people and locked me up."

"But certainly you called your wife and told her what had happened?"

"They wouldn't let me call anybody for six hours," Waldron said. "Not until a little after eight the next morning."

"They refused you permission to telephone your wife?"

"They wouldn't even let me call the union so I could get a lawyer," Waldron said.

"Did the police give any reason for their behavior?"

"They said that the law was when a drunk was brought in, they locked him up for six hours to sober up."

"And did you protest that you were sober?"

"You bet I did," he replied.

"And what did the police say when you protested?"

"They said they had my blood test, and that proved I was drunk," he said.

"Tell me, Mr. Waldron, have you any idea why your blood test would show that you were drunk, after you had, as you said, only two beers?"

"The only reason I can figure is that they got my blood mixed up with somebody else's blood."

"It didn't run through your mind that just possibly the driver of the car with whom you had the collision had some highly placed friends in the police department?"

"It run through my mind, sure," Waldron said. "But you can't prove nothing like that."

"Your Honor, I must most strongly object!" Howell said, jumping to his feet.

"Mr. Davies, you have been warned before," the judge said. "Someone of your legal experience knows full well when a witness is being led. The jury is instructed to disregard both the question and the response. You are not to consider it in your deliberations. And I'm putting you on warning, Mr. Davies. The next time I'll cite you for contempt of court!"

"I humbly beg the court's pardon," Mr. Davies said smoothly. "I have no further questions of Mr. Waldron. Your witness, Counselor."

"I . . . uh . . ." Howell said, getting to his feet, showing disgust on his face, raising his hands in a gesture of disgust and futility. "I cannot see where the interests of truth and justice would be served by asking this man any questions."

"When I went to law school," Mr. Davies said, "I was taught that the way to challenge a witness's testimony was by cross-examination."

"And I was taught," Howell snapped back, "that every once in a long while, you'll have a witness you know is lying through his teeth, but whom you couldn't shake in eight hours of cross-examination."

"That's enough!" the judge almost shouted. "The both of you know better than to engage in an exchange like that. I will not tolerate it!"

"I'm sorry, Your Honor," Howell said.

"I apologize, Your Honor," Davies said.

"Get on with your case, Mr. Davies," the judge said.

"The defense rests, Your Honor," Davies said.

"Are you prepared to give your closing argument?"

"Yes, sir."

"Proceed," the judge said.

Mr. Davies didn't give a long speech, not more than four or five minutes. All he really talked about was how the state had to prove that Mr. Waldron was guilty; that he didn't have to prove that Waldron was innocent. He said that they all had to decide, all twelve of them, that Waldron was guilty beyond any reasonable doubt. He said something about our system of law being based on the principle that it is far better to see a guilty man go free than to convict an innocent man. He said they really had to decide whether or not Mr. Waldron had been fairly accused, and whether or not the State had proved he was guilty. He felt sure, he said, that as reasonable people, seeking justice for everybody, that they would conclude that an unfortunate accident, between a rich young man driving a $20,000 Mercedes home from a tavern and an ordinary citizen driving a Ford home from work had occurred, and nothing more. There was no proof that Mr. Waldron had done any of these things of which he was accused.

Mr. Howell spoke next, and he didn't take long, either. I thought he did the better job. He started out by saying that the only thing the jury was supposed to decide was whether or not he had been able to prove just two things, that Mr. Waldron had run the stop light, and that he had been driving an automobile after he'd had too much to drink.

"You've heard the waitresses in the Quick'n'Ezy," Howell said. "They didn't know either Mr. Waldron or Keith Stevens. They had no interest in this case at all. Both of them swore, under oath, that they saw Mr. Waldron run the stop sign.

"You've heard the police officers testify, under oath, that they thought Mr. Waldron was drunk, and that that was the reason he was asked to submit to a blood test. And you've heard Dr. Sauer testify that the blood sample he took from Mr. Waldron proved beyond any question at all that he was drunk.

"I'm sure the judge will instruct you to judge this case on the facts alone," Howell said. "And on the facts alone, I'm sure that you will return a verdict of guilty."

Then the judge charged the jury. What he did was explain, as well as he could, the fine points of the law involved. He did tell the jury that they weren't supposed to consider any of their personal prejudices, but to decide the case on what they had heard in court, and on nothing else.

Then they were led out of the room. When Mrs. Stevens, Helen, and I walked out of the courtroom, Keith was waiting for us, standing in the middle of the wide marble corridor on his crutches.

"Can you imagine the nerve of that guy?" he said angrily. " 'They got my blood mixed up with somebody else.' I hope they throw him in jail for a year for lying!"

"Now, it's all over, dear," Mrs. Stevens said. "I'm sure the jury could see right through him."

Mr. Howell, the assistant district attorney, walked up to us

"What happens now?" Keith asked. "How long will it take for them to make up their minds?"

"No telling," Mr. Howell said. "In any event there's no use sticking around. Even if they find him guilty—"

"*If?*" Keith asked incredulously.

"If, Keith," Howell said. "Davies did a first-class job of defending him."

"He sure did," Keith said sarcastically. "I was waiting for the judge to pin a medal on that guy, and to apologize for having inconvenienced him."

"That's the way the system works, Keith," Howell said. "Anyway, even if they find him guilty, the judge won't sentence him today. There's what they call a presentencing investigation that comes first. You might as well go home."

"When will we know?"

"I'll call and let you know," he said. He shook our hands, and then we went out of the courthouse and reclaimed the station wagon from the parking garage and drove home. Because her house was on the way, I let Helen off first, then Keith and his mother, and finally I drove home alone.

The whole family, including Barbara, was sitting, dressed up, in the living room, obviously waiting for me.

"We were about to give up on you," my father said. "Lucky you're dressed up. For a change."

"What's up?"

"We're going out for dinner," he said. "Unless you've got homework or something?"

I had something, of course—the suspicion that as soon as Keith had a beer and calmed down, he would get on the telephone and summon the chauffeur. "Not a thing," I said. I had had about enough of Keith for one day.

We all crowded, the six of us, into Paul's Pontiac—Larry, Barbara, and Pop in the front; Paul, Aunt Rose, and me in the back. We headed back to Newark.

"Where are we going?" I asked.

"The VFW," Pop said. "It's Lasagna Night." Lasagna Night meant all the lasagna you could eat for $3.00.

"My father is the last of the big spenders," Paul said to Barbara.

"It's high time she learned she's joining a family of poor cops, and that she shouldn't get the wrong idea, even if some people are driving fancy Pontiacs," Pop said.

"I like lasagna," Barbara said.

It was Lasagna Night, all right, but that wasn't the real reason we were all going to the VFW. When we went into the upstairs dining room, the manager led us past all the people in the main room to one of the side rooms, and when he slid open the door, I saw that it was set up for a special party. There were two signs painted on rolls of white butcher paper. One said "Good Luck, Larry & Barbara" and the other one said "A Romance Born in

Jail." Larry's and Paul's friends were giving Larry and Barbara a prewedding party.

There must have been sixty people in there, one big table holding maybe twenty people, and four-place tables holding the rest. I found myself sitting with Paul and one of his pals from the vice squad and his wife. The wife was pregnant, very pregnant, and it ran through my mind that in a year or so, I was likely to be an uncle.

CHAPTER 15

There was an antipasto, which is an Italian word meaning "before the pasta, or spaghetti or lasagna or whatever, and a bottle of Chianti was sitting in the middle of the table. I turned over my glass and poured it full.

"Well, look at little Allan helping himself to the booze," Mel Shavelson, Paul's friend from vice, said.

"In case you hadn't noticed," Paul said, "little Allan ain't so little no more. And besides he's entitled, he spent the day in court."

"Yeah, so I heard," Mel said.

"What do you mean by that?"

"You haven't heard?" Mel asked.

"Heard what?"

"If you were a big-time lawyer named Davies, defending a guy against a DWI, said guy having enough booze in his blood so that you could set it on fire, what defense would you use?"

"I don't know," Paul said suspiciously.

"You would try to convince the jury that it was a bum rap," Shavelson said.

"How?" Paul asked.

"You tell him, Allan," Shavelson said. "It makes me sick."

"Allan?" Paul demanded.

"He kept bringing up that Keith's mother and Pop are friends," I said.

"Oh, God!" Paul said.

"With the plain suggestion that the only reason those traffic guys gave Waldron the blood test was because he'd run into the Chief's girl friend's kid," Shavelson said.

"I told you that friend of yours was trouble!" Paul snapped at me.

"Makes you sick," Shavelson said. "That's the fourth time they've had that guy on DWI."

"You mean Mr. Waldron's been arrested before?" I asked.

"Oh, has he been arrested before!" Shavelson said. "That's the major reason the DA wanted to get him tried quick. You can't introduce that during the trial, but once there's a conviction, it comes out during the presentencing investigation."

"Why didn't Howell bring that out in court?" I asked.

"I just told you, Allan, you can't bring it out during the trial. It would influence the jury. Now just why the jury shouldn't be influenced is something I don't really understand," Shavelson said. "But that's the way it is."

"Mel, honey," Mrs. Shavelson said, "we're at a party. Won't this keep?"

"Sorry, sweetheart," Shavelson said, and patted her hand.

Paul gave me a dirty look. For some reason, he blamed the whole thing on me.

But we did stop talking about it. They served the lasagna, and afterward they gave Larry and Barbara a bunch of presents, some of them jokes, like baby rattles and a pair of handcuffs in case she couldn't keep him home after they got married, and things like that, and then an unbelievable set of luggage. There were eleven different suitcases and women's makeup boxes and the like.

"We started out collecting money to buy them a good suitcase," Shavelson said, "and they got more than they expected. Somebody, Tony Gregg, I think, decided that since they had collected money for luggage, it had to be luggage. So luggage it is."

"Larry can get all of his clothes in one of the little ones," Paul said. "I don't know about Barbara." But he was as pleased as I was to see what Larry's friends thought of him.

The party didn't last that long. We left about ten-thirty. Paul didn't go home with us. He was going on duty at midnight, and he said he would stick around drinking coffee until then.

Everybody else was in a good mood, and I knew that they hadn't heard yet that Davies's defense had been to suggest that Pop, and Larry too, were the worst kind of cops, the ones that fix things. I thought for a while that when we got home I would get Pop alone and tell him what had happened, so that he wouldn't hear it from somebody else, but I just didn't have the heart to ruin a good evening. So I just said good night and went to bed.

When I got to Keith's house the next morning, Mrs. Stevens met me at the door, looking embarrassed.

"I think I really should have called you," she said. "Keith's a little sick."

"What's wrong with him?" I asked. Before she could answer, Keith shouted at me, "Is that you, Al Capone?"

Not meeting my eyes Mrs. Stevens stepped away from the door and let me in. I went up the stairs to his bedroom. The minute I stepped inside, I could smell why he was sick. The place smelled more like a saloon than the bar at the VFW. A wastebasket by his bed was actually overflowing with empty beer bottles.

"Don't look so righteous," Keith said. "I've already gotten the 'Oh, Keith, how could you?' business from mother."

"What was the occasion?" I asked.

"The occasion was that my bosom buddy deserted me in my hour of need," he said. "Where the hell were you last night, anyway?"

"I went to a party," I said suddenly angry. "I didn't realize that I was on call."

"So I had a few beers all by myself," he said, starting to get out of bed.

"You're still drunk," I said, not so much an accusation as a statement of fact.

"So far as I know, there is no law against drunks walking on crutches," he said.

"They won't let you in school," I said.

"That's what I've been trying to tell him," Mrs. Stevens said softly behind me.

"All I need is one bottle of beer," he said. "A little of the dog that bit me."

"Keith!" Mrs. Stevens said.

"Absolutely not," I said. "They'll throw you out of school, dummy."

"What am I supposed to do?" he asked. "Stay here all day?"

"You just lie back down and get some sleep," I said. "Sober up."

"I think I'd rather have another beer," he said. He reached for his crutches. I grabbed them away from him.

"No way," I said.

"Fine pal you are," he said, but he lay back against the head of the bed.

"You can have the crutches back after school," I said. "You sleep it off, and then we'll stick you in the bathtub."

"Allan's right, dear," Mrs. Stevens said. "Listen to him."

"You're both treating me like a child," he said angrily.

"I'm treating you like a drunk," I said. "And you're in no condition to do anything about it."

"You really think I'm drunk, Al Capone?" He asked the question like a little boy.

I said, "I think you're hung over, and I think you should stay in bed."

"I defer to your wisdom," he said. "Just leave the crutches, and leave me alone."

"I think we'll give you the crutches back when you feel better," I said.

"What if I have to go to the bathroom?" he asked.

"Crawl," I said. "You start staggering around on those crutches, and you'll wind up with both legs in a cast."

"God will get you for this, Al Capone," he said. He looked up at me, and gave me a little smile. "But you may be right. When you get right down to it, I am not really in the mood for American History II this morning, not to mention calculus."

"I'll be over after school," I said.

Mrs. Stevens followed me back downstairs to the door.

"Allan," she said, very embarrassed, "you won't say anything about this to anyone, will you? I mean, people wouldn't understand, I'm afraid."

I knew by people that she meant my father.

"No, I won't say anything," I said.

"He'll be all right after he gets a little sleep," she said. "I just don't believe he knew how much he was drinking."

I had a nasty thought. A reply came to my mind. "He should have guessed when he couldn't get any more beer bottles in the wastebasket." But I didn't say it, of course. I just nodded at her. She leaned up and kissed my cheek. "You're really a friend, Allan," she said.

On the way to school, and in class, when I thought it over, I thought I knew why he'd gotten drunk. He hadn't liked the session on the witness stand, and he had been disgusted when, after testifying, he'd been allowed to hear Mr. Waldron testify. Testify? Lie through his teeth and get away with it!

And who was I to be righteous, anyway? I was feeling pretty good myself by the time Larry's and Barbara's party was over. I'd fallen asleep in the car, and the cold truth of the matter was, I was a little hung-over myself.

Mrs. O'Neill, who taught calculus and analytic geometry, told me in class to come by after school, and she would give me an assignment for Keith so he could keep up with the class. She got hung up with some other teacher, so I had to wait about half an hour for her, and I was maybe forty-five minutes later than I normally would have been when I got to Keith's house.

There was a fire-engine red Pinto in the driveway when I got there, and when I rang the doorbell, Marilyn opened the door.

"Where have you been?" she asked. "Keith's been waiting for you."

"Well, I'm sorry as hell about that," I snapped back at her. "But I had to stop by the harem first, to keep the girls happy."

"Thanks a lot for calling me last night, and telling me what happened," she said. And then she turned and marched into the house. She was stamping her feet in anger as she walked, which made her sort of shake. It was not an entirely unpleasant sight.

I was not at all surprised to see Helen sitting on the couch beside Keith, holding his hand, when I walked into the recreation room. He had his leg resting on a stuffed leather hassock, and he was still in his pajamas and bathrobe.

"Al Capone," he said. "Better late than never."

"Here's a little note from Mrs. O'Neill," I said a little sarcastically. "She said to tell you she was very sorry you're sick."

"Twenty-four-hour virus," he said, and after a moment I realized that he had told the girls this, and I was supposed to go along with it.

"Twenty-four bottles of beer is more like it," I said. I felt Marilyn's eyes on me, and a look on her face that told me she understood suddenly.

"Allan!" Helen said to me. Her voice was hurt that I should make such an unfounded accusation about such an all-around sterling character and victim of society's unjustice.

"Now," Keith said. "If you ladies will kindly leave the room a moment, Allan will put my pants on for me, and then we can go get a hamburger or something."

"Do you really think you should?" Helen asked.

"One thing at a time," Keith said. "Yes, I really think I should put my pants on."

Helen giggled. Then she got up and with Marilyn walked upstairs.

"You've got pants down here?"

"What I need is a beer," he said. "The pants are upstairs. The beer's out in the garage."

"The garage?" I asked.

"There's an extra refrigerator out there," he said. "Mother took the beer out of here and put it out there. She knows I can't make it up those steps with this damned cast."

"You don't need any beer," I said. "You're still in bad shape from last night."

"For God's sake, Allan," he said, and there was genuine anguish in his voice. "Can't you see I'm desperate? For God's sake, get me a lousy beer!"

He had looked all right when I came in. Now he didn't. I realized, with something that might have been horror, that not only didn't he look all right now, but that he really needed a beer.

"Please," he said. It was almost a whine.

I went out into the garage and found the refrigerator and took a bottle of beer from it. Then I went back in the rec room and gave it to him. I didn't look at him. I couldn't. I was embarrassed, although I don't suppose there's any reason I should have been embarrassed; he was the one begging for a beer.

Then I went upstairs and got his pants, and the rest of the stuff he needed to get dressed, and went back down to the recreation room. The beer bottle was nowhere in sight. Keith was standing up on the crutches, getting out of his pajamas. I helped him get dressed. The minute he was finished, he headed for the stairs.

"I'm decent, girls," he called. "No need to avert your eyes. And it's hamburger time."

"I don't want a hamburger," Helen said.

"I do," he said. "Take pity on me, fair maiden."

"Okay," she said.

I wasn't at all surprised when His Royal Highness directed his male nurse and chauffeur to "take a run up the mountain, Al Capone. Ernie's has the best burgers in twenty miles."

He ate a hamburger all right, washed it down with two beers, and was about to order a third when I called a halt to it.

"You've got the calculus, Keith," I said. "And I've got two night's homework."

"Whatever you say, Al Capone," he said. "But as for me, a couple of beers in the company of these lovely ladies has it all over calculus."

At his house Helen walked in with him, to say good-bye, and I said "see you" to Marilyn and started the engine.

"Hey," she said, and I rolled the window down. She walked over. "I'm sorry I snapped at you before," she said. "And I'm sorry you think I'm so stupid."

"Stupid? About what?"

"The reason Apeboy was sick today," she said.

"I don't think you're stupid," I said. "I think he is."

"Maybe he's sick," she said. "That's what his mother thinks."

"I think he's right on the edge of being a drunk," I said.

"And so you're looking for an excuse to check out?" she asked. "I wouldn't blame you." I was shocked. It was as if she could read my mind. I had been wondering how long it was until he could take the cast off and I could be turned loose.

"There's more than him boozing it up so much," I said.

"Is there? Is that why you didn't call me last night and tell me what happened?"

"That's not the reason," I said. "I didn't have time to call you. But I don't think I would have if I had had time."

"And you don't want to tell me? None of my business? Thanks a lot."

"It's not your problem," I said. "That's not the same thing."

"If it's bothering you," she said, "I want to hear about it."

"I'll call you tonight," I said.

"Better still, why don't you come over?" she asked. "Or were you telling the truth about two night's homework?"

"I don't have a car," I said. "And since I've already decided I'm not going to play chauffeur tonight, I really couldn't drive over in Keith's mother's station wagon."

"And you're a real example of machismo, right, who won't ride in a girl's car?"

"I'll ride in a girl's car," I said, "if you're the girl."

"And what time would it be convenient for me to pick you up?" she asked, at the same time mocking me and smiling. We were friends again.

"Try seven o'clock," I said. "Just blow the horn, and I'll come out."

"Nice girls don't do that," Marilyn said. "If you're going to ride in my car, you're going to have to let your family have a look at me."

"Okay," I said.

"See you at seven," she said, and walked over to her car and got in. She blew the horn. The Keith-Helen farewell was getting a little over long.

"Hey," I called, remembering. "You don't know where I live."

"Yes, I do," she said. "I asked."

Then I started the engine again, backed out the driveway, and went home.

My father's absence explained Mrs. Stevens's absence at her house. They were, my aunt Rose said, driving into New York for dinner. That meant it was a big date. Although New York is only twenty, twenty-five miles away (you can see it from Keith's house) people like us don't go there very often. It's as if it's a hundred miles away, in another country.

Larry and Paul were there for supper. Barbara, according to Larry, was spreading truth and light in the slammer.

"Pardon me for asking," Paul said, "but once the pink mist of true love fades a little bit, are you two going to have a conflict of interest? With her trying to get them out of the slammer as fast as you can put them in?"

"No," Larry replied very seriously. "She's actually very practical about it. The ones she's trying to save are generally the ones I hate to see go in. The ones who made a mistake and can be straightened out. With help. Maybe one in five or one in ten. Barbara's not your typical do-gooder."

"I'll defer judgment, if you don't mind," Paul said.

"It may come as a great shock to you, but I don't care what you think," Larry said. "The thing is, she's made me do a little thinking."

"You don't say!" Paul replied sarcastically.

"Yeah, wise guy, I do say. For what it costs us to keep three guys locked up, we can hire one qualified case worker, or probation officer, to keep people outside. And if they're outside, they're working and paying taxes, not eating them up."

"I see that she has got to you," Paul said.

"You guys on vice have a distorted view of society," Larry said. "Even Pop'll tell you that."

"To change the subject, what about Pop? Is he serious about Mrs. Stevens?"

"I don't think that's any of your business," Larry said.

"He's my father, isn't he? That makes it my business."

"No, it doesn't," Larry said. "Be happy for him. I like her."

"I like her, too," Paul said. "It's her kid that bothers me. Pop was pretty upset when he heard what Davies used as a defense."

I was a little ashamed of myself when I didn't jump to Keith's defense.

"Pop wasn't born yesterday," Larry said. "That's a fairly standard procedure. If a cop is involved, personally, there's always a suggestion of unfair influence."

"But Pop wasn't involved."

"I think the jury'll figure that out, too," Larry said. "My God, Waldron had enough alcohol in his blood . . . what did Shavelson say? So that it would burn. I can't see that jury turning him loose."

Larry was wrong.

At 7:01, I was watching the clock, I heard wheels in the driveway and a couple of moments later the doorbell rang and Marilyn was standing in the doorway.

"Come on in," I said, "and brace yourself to meet my brothers."

But even though I said that, I led Marilyn into the kitchen first to meet Aunt Rose. They said hello to each other and Marilyn accepted a piece of cake, and then Larry came in the kitchen.

"Who was that at the door?" he asked, and then he saw Marilyn and his eyebrows went up and a big-brother smirk appeared on his face. Then the phone on the wall rang and he answered it.

"Lieutenant Corelli," he said. And then his face furrowed as he listened. Finally he said, "Yeah, I'll pass the word, Lenny. Thanks for calling." He turned to me. "The judge just dismissed the jury," he said bitterly. "They were deadlocked."

"What's that mean?" Aunt Rose said.

"It means that there was at least one, and maybe more than one, cop-haters on that jury," he said. "But if Waldron thinks he's gotten off again, he's got another think coming. The DA told me that if anything like this happened, he'd have Waldron back in court so fast for a second trial he'd think he was in a revolving door."

"You mean, they turned the man who ran into Keith free?" Marilyn asked.

Larry looked at her as if he was seeing her for the first time.

"Marilyn, this is Larry," Aunt Rose said. "Allan's oldest brother. Larry, this is Marilyn Withers. Allan's friend. Allan's and Keith's."

"Hello," Larry said. "Yeah. that's just what it means," he said, and then he pushed open the door to the dining room again. "Hey, Paul. Hung jury. El Boozerino's off the hook. At least temporarily."

"Oh, no!" I heard Paul say, and then he came storming into the kitchen. "Was that what the doorbell—" He stopped when he saw Marilyn. "Well," he said, and beamed all over. "How long have you been working in the DA's office?"

"She doesn't work in the DA's office," Larry said. "She's Allan's girl friend."

I had been thinking along those lines myself, and I suppose that maybe Marilyn had too, but this was the first time it had been said out loud. I saw Marilyn's face get red, and I realized mine was a little red, too.

"You have all of the feelings of a buffalo," Aunt Rose snapped. "Shame on you. Excuse him, Marilyn."

"It's all right," Marilyn said.

"I didn't mean anything wrong." Larry said lamely.

"What about the Waldron trial?" Paul asked.

"Lenny Faulk just called. The jury was hung. The judge sent them back in three times, and from what Lenny said, was about as mad as I am. But no dice. They were hopelessly deadlocked. He just dismissed them. Waldron's walking."

"Somebody on that jury doesn't like cops," Paul said. "They had him cold. Witnesses, a point-two-one-five concentration of alcohol in his blood. The whole shmear. It makes me sick to my stomach. Will the DA try it again?"

"You bet he will," Larry said. "I just hope he's not mad enough to decide to try it himself."

"Why not? Maybe he could get a conviction," Paul said.

"Because he's Pop's old buddy, that's why," Larry said. "Figure it out for yourself."

"I forgot about that," Paul said. "Under those circumstances. . . ."

I saw that Marilyn, who was listening intently, was confused.

"What Waldron's lawyer did, Marilyn," I said, "was to suggest to the jury that the only reason Waldron was arrested, the only reason they were prosecuting him, was because he ran into Keith, and Keith's mother is sort of running around with my father."

"That's rotten!" she exploded. "That's really dirty!"

"It's a cold, cruel world, honey," Larry said. "It worked. This time."

"There will be another trial?" Marilyn asked.

"You bet there will," Larry said. "And this time Howell had better pick his jury with a lot more care than he did before. Or he'll be prosecuting people who haven't curbed their dogs." He turned to me. "Is your pal home, Allan?"

"Keith, you mean? Yeah, I'm sure he is."

"I'll call him and tell him, so he can tell his mother when she gets home."

"Would it be all right if Allan and I told him?" Marilyn asked.

"Yeah, sure," Larry said. "It might even be better. Allan can explain what's happened as well as I can, and Allan isn't a cop."

"Let's go then," Marilyn said to me.

We got as far as the front door before Larry called after Marilyn.

"Hey, Marilyn," he said. "Two things. First, it was nice to meet you and come again."

"Thank you, I will," she said.

"And second, Allan has such lousy manners that he probably forgot to invite you to my wedding, right?"

"I haven't been invited," she said.

"You have now," Larry said.

"I accept," she said. "Thank you."

I still don't know if that was Larry's idea, or whether Aunt Rose set it up.

CHAPTER 16

When Marilyn turned into Keith's driveway, I was surprised to see that the door of the Mercedes was open. For a moment I wondered if we had come across someone stealing it, for Mrs. Stevens was in New York City with my father, and Keith, of course, couldn't drive it.

But then I saw his crutches leaning against the fender, and as Marilyn stopped the car, I could make him out inside it. I got out of the Pinto and walked up to him. He had the seat pushed all the way back, and his leg, in its cast, was propped across the transmission tunnel and into the footwell on the passenger's side.

"What the hell do you think you're doing?"

"I'm about to demonstrate mind over matter," he said. "Or at least over plaster."

"You can't drive like that," I said. "You're out of your mind."

"Don't be such a pessimist," he said. "I've just about got it figured out."

"You're sitting sideways," I said.

"Not entirely," he said. "And I can work the gas pedal and brake with my left foot."

"You're half out the door," I said. "Have you considered that? How are you going to close it?"

"That *is* a problem," he said. "But not for tonight. You're here."

"What gross insanity are you up to, Apeboy?" Marilyn asked.

"Riding your girl around in my car, huh?" Keith asked.

"No," Marilyn snapped. "He is not. I'm driving my car, and I hope that makes you feel like a fool, because that was a dirty crack."

"I didn't mean anything, for God's sake," he said. "Can't you take a joke?"

"Your jokes aren't too funny," Marilyn said.

"I've apologized. What else do you want me to do?"

"We just heard that there was a hung jury," I said. I was annoyed with him myself for that crack, but Marilyn had told him off at least as well as I could have.

"What do you mean, a hung jury?" he asked.

"They couldn't reach a verdict," I said. "The judge let them go."

"Oh, great. Peachy-keen," Keith said. "The majesty of the law has spoken. It's illegal to run red lights when you're drunk out of your mind, except of course, if you're smart enough to run into a rich kid driving a Mercedes."

"They're going to try him again," Marilyn said. "Larry said so."

"They're not going to get me on that stand again," Keith said. "No way."

"They're not going to ask you, Keith," I said. "They'll subpoena you."

"*Subpoena* me? Listen to Dick Tracy, Junior. I don't care about what they do to me, I'm not going on that stand again."

"Don't be such a spoiled child, Keith," Marilyn said. "Sometimes you're really a pain in—"

"They didn't say, I suppose, why they let him go?" Keith interrupted her.

"They didn't say. They just said they couldn't agree," I said.

"Maybe I will go on the stand again," Keith said, suddenly changing his mind. "I'll get on the stand, and I'll lie through my teeth. I'll swear that I was on my home from a Boy Scout meeting and was driving fifteen miles an hour, because I wanted to be careful with Mommy's car, when I saw him weaving down the street at ninety miles an hour, or better, just before he hit me."

"The only thing you can do is tell the same story over again," I said. "His lawyer will have the transcript of the first trial," I said.

"You saw it, Allan," he said. "How that lawyer made a fool of me, made me look like a real jerk."

"There's nothing you can do about it," I said. "You can bet that Davies is going to want to subpoena you again."

"I'll leave the state," he said.

"Come on, Allan," Marilyn said. "Let's leave him to his self-pity. Maybe with a little bit of luck, he'll be able to get the car started and kill himself, saving a lot of people a lot of trouble."

"Hey, Goofus!" Keith said. "Take it easy. I'm not that bad a guy."

"Sometimes, Keith," she said, "I don't like you at all. This is one of those times."

"Okay, okay, I was out of line. I'm sorry. I really am sorry." He looked up at me. "Hey, Muscles," he said, "you want to pull me out of here? I'm stuck."

I grabbed him under the arms and pulled him out of the car, holding him up until he could get his good foot on the ground under him, and then I hoisted him to his feet.

"Thanks, buddy," he said. Then, quickly, he added, "I guess we'd better go tell Helen, huh?"

"Tell Helen what?" Marilyn asked.

"About the hung jury," Keith said.

I had the feeling that we'd just been maneuvered, but there wasn't anything we could do about it. To tell him to go in the house and telephone the news to Helen would have meant that we would have spurned his apology and were, in addition, leaving him all alone in the cold, cruel world.

With him in the back we couldn't quite close the hatch-back rear end of Marilyn's Pinto. His foot stuck out over the bumper. When I slid in beside her in the front seat, she leaned close, and I could feel her breath on my ear as she whispered something I'm sure Keith felt was romantic. What she said was, "Pray for rain."

Helen gave him the sympathy he was looking for. She interpreted the hung jury as a direct slap at Keith. She also obviously agreed with the notion that making Keith testify again was cruel and unusual punishment and should be unconstitutional.

And we went, of course, to Ernie's, for what I had come to think of as a liquid hamburger, or a hamburger with a head. Marilyn and I got to dance, which was all right, and which gave me the chance to tell her what had happened at the trial, how Davies had tried to paint a picture of the cops leaning on Waldron because of my father. And I told her about Keith getting drunk in his room the night before, and of being too "sick" to go to school.

Marilyn didn't say much. She really didn't have to. I think we both knew we felt the same way about Keith and his boozing. And then, having been pious and outraged about his drinking, and because I was up to my ears in Seven-Up, I ordered a beer for myself. That was a mistake, because even while I was drinking it, Helen announced that she had to get home right then. I gulped it down. We loaded Romeo and Juliet in the back of the Pinto and went back to Springview.

I got dropped off first, probably, I decided, because Marilyn didn't want to give Keith an opportunity to make some kind of crack, and when I walked in the house, my father was sitting on the couch, and I sensed he was waiting for me.

"Home early, aren't you, Dad?" I asked.

"Yeah," he said distractedly. "We didn't get to New York." He stood up and walked over to me. "Come on," he said. "I'll buy you a cup of coffee or a sandwich." Then he sniffed. "You've been drinking beer, huh?"

"I had one beer."

"Come on," he said. We went out and got in his car and headed into downtown Springview. I thought we were headed for the police station.

"Is something wrong?" I asked.

"You know there is," he said. But instead of turning off Gregory Avenue into the spot reserved for the Chief of Police in front of the station, he drove a block further and pulled into the parking lot of the Olde Towne Pump, which was a restaurant in front and a bar in back. We went into the bar, and he propelled me to a booth in the corner. When the waitress came, he ordered a beer.

"You want a beer," too?" he asked.

"Please," I said.

"The waitress gave me sort of a strange look, but I guess she decided that it would be all right to serve me. The Springview cops were not likely to ask the Springview Chief of Police any embarrassing questions about how old I was.

Pop didn't say anything until the beer was delivered. Then he took a sip and sort of attacked me from an angle.

"Where'd you go tonight?"

"A friend of mine picked me up and we went out to Ernie's," I said.

"The same friend your Aunt Rose thinks is a charming young lady?"

"Yeah."

"Don't say 'yeah,'" he said automatically. "And you went to Ernie's for a couple of beers?"

"I had one beer," I said. "Marilyn drank Seven-Up."

"You went alone?"

I knew what he was leading up to. I wasn't about to catch it for drinking a beer.

"No, Keith and his girl were with us."

"And they had a couple of beers?"

"Yes, sir."

"She drinks a lot, does she?"

"I think she drinks because Keith drinks," I said.

"I had a very unpleasant time tonight," Pop said. "I picked up Mrs. Stevens, and we started for New York. But before we even got to Newark, when we were going past Seton Hall, she started to cry."

I didn't say anything. He looked at my face for a moment, and then went on.

"She was pretty unhappy," he said. "She said she really hated to bother me with her problems, but that she had nowhere else to go. And she said that she was ashamed to tell me that she'd put you in a bad spot. I guess you know what she meant."

"I wasn't going to lie to you, Pop," I said. "If you asked."

"Yeah, I know that," he said. "So I'm asking now. Has she got reason to be as upset as she is?"

"Yeah, I think she does," I said. "I don't know what's the matter with him."

"I was afraid for a minute that you'd think I was asking you to squeal on your friend," he said. "I'm glad you understand my position."

"I don't think I'm squealing," I said.

"You know that story about Keith leaving St. Whatsisname's school because his mother wanted him home after his father died?"

"Uh huh."

"It's not true. He got thrown out for drinking."

"Oh," I said.

"Mrs. Stevens told me that tonight," Pop said. "Was he drunk when he punched the coach?"

I had to think about that, but finally I said. "I don't think so, no."

"But he did get drunk at our house?"

I nodded.

"And he was drunk last night?"

"Oh, yeah. His wastebasket was full of beer bottles."

"Tonight?"

"No. He doesn't get drunk when he's with me," I said. It was the first time I'd thought about that. But once I said it, I knew it was true.

"What about at the country club? When he had the fight there?"

"You heard about that, huh?"

"I heard you stopped him before it really got out of hand. I asked, was he drinking then?"

"I don't know for sure," I said. "I was off with Marilyn."

"Off where?"

"Shooting pool, as a matter of fact," I said.

"Is that what they call it these days?" he said, and smiled at me.

"We were shooting pool," I said. "On one of those tables without holes."

"Billiards," he said. "What do you think?"

"Yeah, I think he was drinking. I was. Champagne."

"But you didn't throw anybody into a row of chairs," he said. "So afterward, what happened?"

"I dropped him off at his house and started home," I said. "He caught up with me in the Mercedes coupe. He wanted to go out for a hamburger. I wanted to go home. So he went off by himself."

"Do you know where?" Pop asked.

I thought a moment before replying. I was pretty close to the line between telling it like it was and squealing.

"Paul said he saw the car in front of that Chinese beer joint on Mott Street at midnight," I said.

Pop didn't say anything, but I could tell by the look in his eyes that dumb luck had made me tell the truth about that. I could see that he had already known; Paul had told him.

"So there's a good chance he was drunk, or nearly drunk, when he had the accident," Pop said.

"I don't *know* that," I said. "And neither do you. He could have been playing the ping-pong machine or something."

"You can bet that Davies is going to have a witness at the next

Waldron trial testifying just how long Keith was in that place, and how many beers he had," Pop said. "Well, that can't be helped. The question is, what do we do about Keith?"

"I don't know, Pop," I said.

"I wish you wouldn't call me 'Pop,'" he said. "It sounds disrespectful."

"I don't mean it that way," I said.

"Just don't do it, okay?" he said. I knew this was just a smokescreen. He had been asked by Mrs. Stevens to help Keith, and he didn't have any more idea how to help than I did.

"Sorry," I said.

"I thought it was maybe because his father's dead," Pop said. "But Virginia says that he was drinking before that. And Mr. Stevens wasn't sick or anything. I mean, he just keeled over with a heart attack."

"Maybe he didn't like being sent away to school," I said.

"Have you said anything to him?"

"Have I given him a speech, you mean? No. He knows I get pretty burned up at him. And Marilyn's given him hell, too. She gave him hell tonight."

"He was drunk tonight?"

"He was feeling sorry for himself," I said. "He's afraid of having to testify again."

"He doesn't have any choice in the matter," Pop said. "I talked to the DA. He wants me and Larry to testify, if Davies starts out with that bum rap routine again. And more to the point, he told me that Keith is Davies's best witness. Jurors don't like seventeen-year-old boys driving $20,000 Mercedes automobiles. Even when they're sober and we can count on Davies to imply that he wasn't."

It was obvious that Pop had a double interest in all this. He wanted to do whatever he could for Keith, because of Mrs. Stevens. But he was still—and probably more significantly—a cop who wanted to get Waldron off the highways.

He drained his beer, raised the glass over his head, looked at my half-empty glass, and ordered one more. Then he turned to me.

"Think you could face those driver-education movies again?" he asked.

"Oh, Pop!" I said. The driver-education movies he was talking about were not what probably comes to mind, sort of a training film for high school juniors, showing them what hand to use on the gear shift. The movies Pop was talking about were the ones the state police had made at accidents. If you got arrested for drunken driving (and sometimes for reckless driving) you could sometimes have your sentence reduced (in other words get your suspended license back quicker) if you went to what they called a "Driver Education Program." The program consisted of lectures and the movies. The movies showed what happened to people when two cars collided head on or when they ran into a bridge support. Things like that. There was one scene I'll never forget as long as I live. A guy in a sports car had run off the highway and under a barrier. The steel cables of the barrier had taken off his windshield and his head. I'll never forget those full-color movies of the headless body, covered with blood, still behind the wheel. And the head lying in a drainage ditch with the eyes still open.

One of the privileges of being a senior police officer's son was getting to see the driver-education movies without having to get yourself arrested for drunken driving. I saw them the day I got my driver's license, my father being one of those who believes an ounce of prevention is worth a pound of cure.

"It might work," Pop said. "You got any better ideas?"

I started to say something and stopped. Pop caught it.

"Let's hear it," he said. And then when I still didn't say anything, he said. "He's your friend, and he's in trouble."

"What about AA," I said. "Alcoholics Anonymous."

"I brought that up," my father said. "Not AA, but Alateen, which is geared specially for young people. They do great work. But you need something for them to work with."

"I don't follow you," I said.

"You have to go to them admitting you have a problem," my father said. "And it really helps if your family is willing to admit that you have a problem. Neither Keith nor his mother are willing to admit his problem is that bad." He looked at me. "What about you? Could you talk him into going?"

I thought it over. There was no way I could talk Keith into doing something like that. I finally shook my head no.

"Then it's the driver education movies," my father said. "That's *something*."

"Why do I have to see them again? I was impressed the first time I saw them. I'm a true believer."

"Well, he can hardly walk to the state police barracks," my father said. "And he is, I think, your friend."

"How are you going to get him to go?"

"I promised Virginia I'd have a talk with him," Pop said, a little embarrassed. "His own father's dead. You know."

"I don't know, Pop," I said. "It may work."

"Intelligent people are supposed to be able to learn from other people's mistakes," he said. "I think it's worth trying."

"When are you going to talk to him?" I asked.

"First thing in the morning," he said. "You take my car to school. I'll pick Keith up in their station wagon, have a talk with him, and then swap cars in the parking lot at school."

"You'll have to put his pants on," I said.

"It wouldn't be the first time I've put pants on a young man," Pop said. "Come on, let's get out of this joint before Rose gets all over me for corrupting your morals."

CHAPTER 17

Keith and I didn't have any morning classes together. I didn't see him until I walked into the cafeteria for lunch. I was also, of course, his tray carrier. It's hard to carry a tray when you're on crutches. That meant I had to go through the line twice. By the time I got back to the table with my tray, he had finished his.

"I understand we're going to the movies," he said. "I guess you know about it?"

"Yeah, I know about it," I said.

"Are you an innocent victim of circumstance, or part of the conspiracy to reform Keith?" he asked.

"Both, I suppose," I said. "I think you need reforming, but I'm a victim, too. I can do without a replay of those movies."

"That bad, huh?" he asked. "You think it will work? Reform me?"

"If you're smart, it will make you think about how much you drink before you drive."

"You sound just like your old man," he said. "I can't wait to see them."

"Just to set the record straight," I said, "my father's not putting his two cents in your business because he wants to. Your mother asked him to."

"So she said," Keith said. "I think you're all a little hysterical."

"You get so drunk you can't go to school, and we're hysterical?"

"When I got drunk," he said, "it was the first time in the long history of the world that happened?"

"The *third* time," I said, getting a little hot under the collar. "The first time got you thrown out of that fancy school you went to. The second time was when you got sick at my house. Okay?"

"What do all of you want from me, anyway?" he asked.

"I don't want anything from you," I said. "What your mother wants, for reasons that escape me, is to keep you alive."

"And your father? What's his angle?"

"I don't think he wants you running over the citizens with a load on," I said.

"I am surrounded by noble people," he said. "I suppose I should be flattered."

"Look," I said. "I was not asked about this. I was told."

"Your father explained why I have to testify again," he said.

"Don't change the subject," I said. "Has it ever occurred to you that you might be an alcoholic?"

"Don't be ridiculous!" he snapped.

"What's ridiculous about it? You can't handle it. And, boy, you really needed something to drink when your mother put the beer in the garage. You were begging for it."

"Go to hell, Allan," he said. "Butt out of my business."

"I wish I could," I said angrily. "But like you said, I'm an innocent victim of circumstance."

He pushed himself to his feet, nearly knocking the table over as he did, grabbed his crutches, stuck them under his arms, and hobbled out of the cafeteria.

CHAPTER 18

There was a large, blank-faced, young state trooper sitting behind a window in the wall of the headquarters building of the trooper barracks when we walked in.

"You the two for the driver-ed films?" he asked, before I could open my mouth.

"That's right."

"Hey, Tom," he called over his shoulder. "I've got to show the movies. You want to take over for me?" He got to his feet, and another trooper took his place. The young one came through a door, made a gesture with his hand for us to follow him, and led us into the building.

He led us to a classroom. A projector and a screen had been set up.

"You want to close the blinds, pal?" he said to me. "And you sit down," he said to Keith. "What did you do to your leg?"

"I was in an auto accident," Keith said.

"No fooling?" he said sarcastically, arrogant. "I never would have guessed."

As soon as I had pulled the last blind in place, he started the projector. I had to find a place to sit down in the dark. I had told myself that the second time around it wouldn't be as bad as it was the first time. I was wrong. Gruesome is gruesome. I played a little game of chicken with myself. Even knowing what was coming, I proved that I was tough and manly by keeping my eyes open. I didn't get sick to my stomach, which I thought was a real possibility, but I came close; I had a clammy sweat.

There were three reels in all, each about thirty minutes long. I didn't look over my shoulder at Keith when the trooper turned the lights on to change reels. I just looked at the little beads in the screen and waited until the lights went off and the next reel came on.

Finally the last reel was over.

"That's it," the young trooper said. "If you feel like tossing your cookies, the men's room is across the hall."

When I looked over my shoulder, Keith was already on his way out of the room, and I realized that he was probably going to throw up. So I took my time leaving the room, and when I got out in the hall, I took a long drink of water waiting for Keith to come out of the men's room.

"Hey, Allan, how are you?" a voice called, and I came up from

bending over the water fountain to see Captain Ropke, the barracks commander, and an old friend of my father's.

"Hello, Captain Ropke," I said. "How are you?"

"Your Dad called me about sending you over," he said. "They
taking care of you all right?" He put his arm around my shoulder
as he shook my hand. The nasty trooper came out of the classroom as he did so. He did a double take and for the first time,
smiled.

"Thanks for showing us the film," I said.

"Allan's an old friend of mine," Captain Ropke said. "I still hope
to get him to see that the only way to be a cop is to be a trooper."

"I couldn't do that, Captain," I said. "I get sick at wrecks."

"We all do," Captain Ropke said. "That's the hell of it."

Keith came out of the men's room. He didn't look to me like
he'd been sick.

"And you're Stevens, I suppose?" Captain Ropke said. "Chief
Corelli told me what a hard time Davies gave you. I'm Captain
Ropke."

"How do you do?" Keith said, shaking his hand.

"Hey, fellas," the nasty trooper said. "I read you guys wrong.
I thought you were a couple of punks that the Captain was trying
to straighten out."

"Just one of us," Keith said. "Just one of us."

Captain Ropke gave him a look, and then said. "You guys want
a Coke? Or a cup of coffee?"

"I'd like one, please," Keith said. "Those movies are something
else."

"They're pretty grim," Captain Ropke said. "When we show
them to recruits, we can count on at least one in the class getting
sick."

"They make you think," Keith said.

Captain Ropke led us to a sort of living room, used by the troopers who lived in the barracks, and there were Coke machines and a couple of coffee makers. We drank a cup of coffee, and then Captain Ropke walked with us to the parking lot.

"See you Sunday," he said. "Tell your father that the wife and I are looking forward to the wedding, even if it makes us feel kind of old."

When we were in the station wagon heading back to Spring-view, Keith said, "Speaking of the wedding. . . ."

"What about it?"

"How much in the way would Helen be if she came?"

"The more the merrier," I said, without even thinking about it. "You think she'd want to come?"

"The allegedly gentle sex are wedding freaks," Keith said. "I'm surprised you don't know that. You did ask Marilyn?"

"My brother did," I said.

"Well?"

"I'm sure she'd be welcome," I said. "If only because you're likely to stay at least reasonably sober if she's there."

"Hey, lay off, will you? I've been converted."

"To what?"

"If I tell you, you'll either laugh or be awful self-righteous."

"Tell me anyway," I said.

"I don't believe for a minute what you said about there being a chance that I'm an alcoholic," Keith said. "But on the other hand, let's face it, I have been drinking a little too much."

"What I don't understand is why," I said.

"Huh?"

"What I mean is that most people get bombed by accident. You seem to do it on purpose."

"You've lost me," Keith said.

"You don't want to follow me," I said. "You know what I mean. You drink to get drunk, not to have a good time. And I mean to get drunk, not just high."

"I wasn't aware that you were a psychiatrist," Keith said.

"All I'm saying is that you do it, and you know you do it, and I don't understand why."

"Who knows?" he said, suddenly serious. "Sometimes, I guess, I simply would rather be drunk than sober. Maybe it's because of my father...." He stopped. I could tell he wasn't going any further.

"So what are you going to do about it?" I said. "Now that we're agreed you're drinking a little too much lately."

"So what I think I'm going to do is prove to myself, and you too, that I'm not an alcoholic."

"How are you going to do that?"

"I'm going to go on the water wagon," he said. "For six months."

"Starting when?"

"Starting now," he said. "From right now, booze will never pass these handsome lips of mine for six months. One hundred and eighty days."

"The movies got to you, huh?" I said.

"They didn't get to you?" he asked.

"I almost threw up the first time I saw them," I said. "And I almost threw up now."

"I don't suppose you'd want to join me on the water wagon?" he asked. "To lend me a little moral support?"

"I don't know," I said, and then I thought about it. "No, why should I? I don't get falling down drunk. I don't get sick."

"Okay," he said. "Have it your way. If I can watch you throw down the filthy stuff, and maintain my noble intentions, that would prove that I can take it or leave it alone, wouldn't it?"

"I suppose it would," I said. "I just hope this lasts through Sunday. I don't want you getting bombed and ruining Larry's wedding reception."

"Put your mind at rest, Al Capone," Keith said. "While everybody else is getting fall-down drunk, I shall be a splendid example of the absolute teatotaler."

"Nobody's going to get fall-down drunk," I said.

"Nonsense," he said. "No wedding reception can be considered a success unless somebody—hopefully the bride or the groom—gets bombed out of his or her mind. It gives people something to talk about until the next tribal ritual."

It wasn't true, of course, but I laughed with him. I guess what I felt was an enormous sense of relief. Pop had said the test of an intelligent person was whether or not he could learn from other people's mistakes. Although he was trying not to show it, the movies had gotten to him. Maybe more than that. He hadn't said anything about what Pop had said to him that morning. My father is an intelligent man, and he understands people. I couldn't even guess as to what he'd said to Keith, but I knew that whatever it was, it had probably made an impression.

"Let's stop by Helen's," he said. "She's a very sensitive girl. With a little bit of luck, I can make her sick to her stomach just telling her about the movies."

"Why not?" I said, and headed toward Helen's house.

We had a house full of people for supper. Larry and Barbara were there, and so were Judge and Mrs. Klaus. Judge Klaus had been sort of the cupid in the great romance, assigning the detective-sergeant son of his old friend to show the do-gooder around the slammer. He had probably done so, I thought somewhat cynically, to keep her from being torn apart by the inmates or thrown out by the guards, who weren't too fond of do-gooders, but now he and everybody else were agreed that he had done so to put Larry and Barbara together, and he sort of liked that.

Anyway, he had been asked to marry them and had agreed, and the reason he was at the house was to check things out for the ceremony. Aunt Rose made a leg of lamb, which is usually something we had only on Sunday, and Pop had brought home some good wine, and the judge and Pop went on a nostalgia kick during dinner, remembering how they had met in night school.

"There was this skinny fellow," the judge told the story, "wearing khaki pants and a sweater. It was a long summer, and everybody was sweating, him too, but he kept the sweater on. Night after night, mind you, not just once. Everybody's sitting there sweating, and there's this chap with a sweater. So one day, my curiosity got the better of me, and when I came across him in the men's room during a break in class, I asked him. 'Excuse me,' I said. 'But aren't you a little warm in that sweater?' "

" 'I'm melting,' he said. So I asked him, 'Why don't you take it off?' So he pulled it up in front, and there's the butt of a large pistol sticking out of the waistband. 'Do you think you need that?' I asked, and he said, 'No, I don't think I need it. But the chief of police does. I'm a cop.' Now, I'll tell you, the last thing in the world that I would have thought about that sweating skinny little chap was that he would be a police officer."

Everybody laughed, although everybody but Barbara had heard the story maybe a dozen times. He left out the part about the pistol being the service revolver, with the six-inch barrel instead of the two-inch snub-nose you could carry off-duty. The story went that Pop couldn't afford the price of a snub-nose.

Anyway they had become friends in night school. The judge was going to law school, and Pop was studying for the sergeant's exam, and the class they were both in was the Laws of Evidence, and they'd been friends ever since. The judge had been an assistant DA for a while, then gone into private practice as a criminal lawyer, and finally been appointed a judge.

With that background I suppose it wasn't surprising that when Aunt Rose, Mrs. Klaus, and Barbara went to the kitchen to do the dishes, and we went in the living room to drink espresso, the conversation turned to the Waldron trial and then to Keith.

"I'm of two minds about it," the judge said. "Maybe three minds, if you bring in our friendship. As a friend, of course, I'm furious at Davies's behavior. He had no shred of evidence to suggest that you were in any way involved in the matter. But put the friendship aside. It's essentially a question of ethics.

"You could say that it was unethical of him to suggest that you were involved, that you had somehow exercised your influence on the arresting officers."

"*Could* say?" Paul said. "It's dishonest, and if it's dishonest, it can't be ethical."

"The minute I heard that the guy Waldron had hit was Allan's buddy from school," Larry said, "I called the office and told them I couldn't touch the case."

"All right, that was ethical behavior on your part," the judge said. "Not commendable, because that's what you were supposed to do. And Davies did what he is supposed to do."

"He's supposed to accuse Pop and me of railroading some guy because the guy he hit is a pal of my baby brother's?" Larry asked.

"He is supposed to provide the accused with the best defense he can," Judge Klaus said. "It's the theory on which the adversary system of justice works."

"I don't mind being an adversary," Paul said. "Which I think means I have to prove my case."

"That's right."

"But how come the scales of justice are tipped in favor of the bad guys?" Paul went on. "Look at this case. Two witnesses, who never heard of Pop or ever saw either the accused or the Stevens kid before in their lives, got up there and testified they saw Waldron run the stop sign, going too fast. And then a doctor gets up and swears there was no question at all, based on laboratory tests, that Waldron was drunk. Now if that isn't open and shut, what is?"

"Come on, Paul," Pop said. "You know you have to prove something beyond a shadow of doubt."

"And I think Howell did. What happened is that some cop-hater on the jury decided that if a cop accused this citizen of something, it gave him a good chance to get back at the cops for laying a speeding ticket on him, or something, three years ago."

"You don't know that to be a fact," the judge said.

"If it walks like a duck, and quacks like a duck . . ." Paul said.

"What really bugs me is why we couldn't let the jury know that this isn't the first time brother Waldron has been accused of driving drunk," Larry said.

"That protects the rights of the accused," Judge Klaus said. "We have to presume him innocent of all charges until the government proves its case."

"And in the meantime, Waldron walks," Larry said. "Or rather drives, probably drunk."

"Now wait a minute," the judge said. "All that Davies was saying to the jury, really, was asking them if they felt the accusations were fair, or whether Waldron had been unjustly accused because of possible police influence."

"Yeah, and all he has to do is make the accusation, and we have to prove it isn't so. It's like asking a guy if he has stopped kicking his dog, answer yes or no. No matter what he says, it looks like he has been kicking the dog, even if he hasn't."

"What if the Stevens boy had been speeding? Or was drunk?" the judge said. "Won't you agree that the interests of justice would be served if the jury knew that?"

"The justice I'm interested in is getting that guy off the road before he kills somebody," Paul said.

"If the jury always took the word of the police, we'd have what they call a police state," the judge said. "If that sounds like a lecture, Paul, I'm sorry."

"Oh, you're right, I know," Paul said. "It just gets a little frustrating at times."

"How did it go today, Allan?" my father asked me.

"All right, I think," I said.

"How did what go today?" Paul asked.

"I had Allan taken Keith over to the state police barracks for the horror movies," Pop explained. "What does 'all right, I think' mean?"

"On the way home he told me he was going to stop drinking for six months, just to prove he can," I said.

"That's progress," Paul said. "You think he can do it?"

"I don't know," I said.

"I gather he does have a drinking problem?" Judge Klaus asked.

"Yes, sir," I said. "I don't think it's too serious."

"For Allan to consider it serious," Paul said, "he'd have to beg for a drink."

Keith's face, as he begged me to get him a beer from the garage, popped into my head. But I didn't say anything.

"A lot of young men drink too much when they first start," Judge Klaus said. "I know I did. You're not suggesting that he's an alcoholic?"

"Just that he drinks entirely too much," my father said. "I think it's probably got something to do with losing his father."

"And maybe he just likes it," Paul said. "The taste *and* the effect."

"You've really got it in for him, don't you?" I asked.

"I'm calling it like I see it," Paul said. "That guy's headed for trouble."

"Let's give him the benefit of the doubt," my father said. "I like him."

Paul looked as if he was going to say something, but didn't.

CHAPTER 19

It looked to me as if it would have been much easier to rent a hall somewhere, say at the Villa Scarlatti, or at the VFW Post, and hold the wedding and the reception there, but Pop and Aunt Rose were determined to see Larry married off in the house.

That meant that I spent most of the rest of the week doing the same things I had done when they had the engagement announcement party—running errands. Mrs. Stevens contributed the use of the station wagon, of course, and the services of Keith. He rode along with me to supervise the loading of chairs and things. So far as I could tell, he didn't even sniff the neck of a beer bottle all week.

On Saturday night we double-dated to the movies. This meant a drive-in, of course, and parking the car very carefully over the hump in the parking area so that Keith could see out from the back seat.

Afterward we went to Ernie's. It was Keith's suggestion, and I frankly wondered whether he figured that he'd been without his beer long enough, four whole days, and that having proved he could do without it, he would have a couple of bottles of beer.

But he didn't. He ordered Seven-Up for himself before any of the rest of us ordered. I decided to test his high resolve and ordered a beer. Marilyn and Helen ordered beer too, but even that didn't seem to bother him at all.

As we were leaving Keith said I should let Helen drive, because she was going to take the station wagon so that she could drive him to our house for the wedding the next day. I got in back with him, Helen got beside Marilyn in the front seat, and I was driven home to be dropped off first. Only after I'd walked in the door did I remember that while Helen could drive the station wagon, she couldn't very well help Keith put his pants on in the morning.

I woke up Sunday morning to hear Pop laughing and Aunt Rose having a fit.

"Oh, Paul," she said. "You'll look awful!"

"I did it on purpose, of course, to ruin the wedding," Paul replied. What had happened was that Paul had tried to arrest a lady who didn't want to be arrested, and who had raked her fingernails over his face.

"Big date last night, huh?" I said to him, and he threatened to do me bodily harm.

Mrs. Stevens appeared then to help out, and she said she

thought she could cover most of the scratches with makeup, and when I went to her house to get Keith dressed, would I bring her makeup kit?

"Yes, ma'am," I said, "with pleasure."

"Thank you very much," Paul said. "But I think I'd rather just look awful."

"Nobody'll be able to tell," Mrs. Stevens said. "At least let me try. If you don't like it, you can wash it off."

"Let her try, Paul," Pop said. "What have you got to lose?"

"Yeah," I said. "Lots of guys wear makeup. Some even carry purses."

"You better get him out of here, Pop," Paul said. So I took Pop's car and went to Keith's house to help him put his pants on. He wasn't sound asleep, as I thought he would be, but rather downstairs, and I had the unpleasant feeling that if I hadn't shown up right then, he would have had a drink. I didn't have reason to feel that way, just the feeling.

So when he told me that Helen was coming over to cook him some breakfast, I stuck around until she showed up. She had Marilyn with her, and they had a suitcase, and the idea was that they were going to amuse Keith until it was time to come over to our place. They would change into dresses at Keith's house.

"What are you doing with that?" Marilyn asked, as I left, pointing at the makeup kit.

"It's for my brother," I said. "He wants to look his best for the wedding. He's best man, you see."

"And you're going to carry the ring on a little pillow, right?" she replied.

When I got back to the house with the makeup kit, and went upstairs, there were three strange women in my bedroom. It had been taken over for Barbara, although she hadn't shown up yet.

When she saw me, Mrs. Stevens took the makeup kit from me and marched Paul into Aunt Rose's bedroom. I wasn't allowed to watch. So I went to my bedroom and got my clothes, and went into Larry's bedroom to get dressed.

Larry and Pop were in there with a bottle of scotch.

"What do you want?" Pop asked.

"There're strange women in my bedroom," I said. "I've got to get dressed someplace."

"Well, get dressed then," he said. I had the feeling that they were having a conversation I wasn't supposed to hear. They waited impatiently for me to put my suit on, and didn't say a word until I had left.

I went downstairs. The place was already filling up with people, and among them was Mr. Howell. That shouldn't have surprised me. He was an assistant DA, and Larry was, after all, a lieutenant on the DA's squad. I had nothing against him, but I was a little sorry to see him there, and then I realized why. Because of Keith.

It was a good guess.

"Is your buddy going to be here?" he asked.

"Yeah, in half an hour or so. Or an hour."

"We got the court calendar juggled," he said. "We're bringing Waldron to trial again on Tuesday."

"Oh?"

"And I had a little talk with Davies. He said that if I personally guaranteed that Keith would be there, he wouldn't insist on serving him with a subpoena. I don't think he wants him spooked any more than necessary. But I am going to have to see him, and today."

"He'll be here," I said. "Could you wait until after the wedding?"

"Just as long as I see him," Howell said.

"There's more to it than the subpoena, isn't there?" I asked.

"All right," Howell said, after he thought about it. "I want to make sure that he doesn't decide to try to help me."

"What do you mean?"

"Sometimes in a situation like this, a witness goes over his testimony and comes up with an idea why he wasn't believed the first time. I don't want Stevens to ... *amplify* his story, if you know what I mean. I want him to know that Davies will have a record, either a tape recording or a transcript, of his testimony. Do you know what I'm talking about?"

"Yeah," I said. "I know what you mean."

Paul came downstairs a few minutes later, looking somewhat sheepish. I decided it was not the time to tell him that Mrs. Stevens's makeup worked. He wouldn't have believed me.

"Where's Pop and Larry?"

"Upstairs having a private conversation," I said.

"Let's check the backyard," he said. The wedding was to be held in the backyard, although the term Aunt Rose was using was "garden." Larry and Barbara would be married in a "garden wedding."

An arch had been set up by a florist, made out of slats, with flowers wired to it. At first the idea had been to put chairs out there, but the lawn was too soft, and the chair legs sank into the ground. So everybody would stand up while the ceremony was held. Barbara's boss was going to give her away, since her father was dead. Paul was going to be Larry's best man, and friends of the both of them would be the ushers. I had no role in the affair at all, except of course, afterward, when I would take things down.

The reception would be held here, and since it was a nice day, another bar had been set up outside. It was discreetly covered with a tablecloth until after the ceremony. Paul headed for it, grabbed two bottles of beer from the cooler, and led me into the basement, where he opened the bottles and handed me one.

"Cheers," he said. "Oddly enough, I think we're going to miss Larry around here."

"Yeah," I agreed.

"I'm sorry Mom's not here to see this," Paul said. "You know. Larry making lieutenant so young and getting a nice girl like that."

I couldn't think of anything to reply to that. It was the most emotional thing I had ever heard Paul say. He didn't stay in that mood long.

"You keep that pal of yours sober, you understand?" he said. "I don't want any problems at all today."

"I told you, he's on the wagon," I said.

"If you haven't seen him in the last sixty seconds, you can't know that," he said. He took a pull at his beer bottle, and at that moment a fat lady in a pink dress and floppy hat opened the door. She had an electric cord in her hand, and she gave the both of us a dirty look. Then she wiggled the cord at us.

"For the organ," she said.

"I beg your pardon?"

"I've got to plug in the organ," she said.

"Oh, sure," Paul said. "Allan will take care of that, won't you, kid?" And then he went further into the basement, and I heard his footsteps on the stairs.

The cord the lady had was long, but not long enough to reach an outlet, so I had to find an extension cord. Then she came back in as I was finishing my beer and said she had to have bricks or something, her chair was sinking into the ground. I couldn't find any bricks, but we tried putting a small rug under the chair, and that worked. She wasn't sitting exactly straight up and down, but she wasn't sinking into the ground either. She started to play the organ, and when I looked at my watch, I saw that it was only fifteen minutes until the wedding itself.

I went into the house. The place was really jammed full of people now. I found Keith, Helen, and Marilyn by the front door. Keith was leaning against the wall. Marilyn and Helen, all dressed up, even hats, looked older than they usually did.

Then Aunt Rose swept through the house, chasing everybody outside. I was afraid that Keith's crutches would sink into the grass the way the legs of the chair had, so I warned him to be careful. We made our way to one of the trees, and he leaned against that and we waited.

It didn't take long. Larry came around the side of the house, looking a little shook, with Paul, who was grinning from ear to ear. As they walked up to the arch, I saw Judge Klaus and looked around for my father. He was standing up in front with Mrs. Stevens.

Then the lady in the pink dress, who had kept looking over her shoulder, turned around, nodded her head, and started playing "Here Comes the Bride." Barbara came around the corner of the house on the arm of her boss, who looked about as nervous as Larry.

"On the whole," Keith whispered too loudly, "I favor elopements."

The girls shushed him.

The ceremony itself didn't take long. Judge Klaus had a firm, loud, and deep voice, and we could hear him all right, but we could barely hear either Larry or Barbara when they responded. But finally Larry put a ring on her finger, Barbara put one on his, they kissed, and that was it.

They turned around and marched through the people, and this

time they came right past us. Larry winked at me. He didn't look
so nervous anymore.

"Another good man gone wrong," Keith said.

"Oh, shut up," Marilyn and Helen said, almost together, but
they didn't seem angry.

Then as they disappeared around the other side of the house,
my father walked quickly up to me.

"We're short a bartender," he said. "I don't know what happened to him. Will you start serving down here, until I find out
what happened?"

"Sure," I said.

"I'll help," Marilyn said. "If you want me to."

"You don't mind?" my father said.

"I'd like to," she said.

"That's very nice of you," he said, and then headed for the
house.

Marilyn and I went to the outside bar, took the tablecloth off,
and started passing out whatever people wanted to drink. There
was champagne and wine, and all kinds of booze. The glasses
were plastic, which had been a source of disagreement between
Aunt Rose and Pop. Pop hadn't liked them, and Aunt Rose said
they were the only thing that made sense. He had given in in the
end.

It quickly became apparent that our bar was going to be for
Larry's and Paul's friends, and that Pop's friends, and the other
older people, were going to do their drinking in the house. Only
about half of our "customers" went inside for the cutting of the
wedding cake, and about half an hour after that, Larry and
Barbara came outside. That was the first chance I got to kiss the
bride.

"They shouldn't be making you work," she said.

"Remember that," I said. "Be nice to the youngest of your kids."

And maybe forty-five minutes after that, Larry and Barbara left. We all went around to the front of the house to throw rice at them. They came running out the house, ducking the rice, and Larry held the door of Barbara's car open for her like a gentleman, and then ran around and got behind the wheel and turned the key.

Then the siren went off. I looked at Paul. He and Mel Shavelson were standing with their arms folded, smiling from ear to ear. It didn't take much to figure out that they had wired a siren to the ignition system. Larry got out of the car, opened the hood, and while everybody applauded, found the wires and ripped them loose. Then he got behind the wheel again, started the engine, and drove off. He got about fifty feet before there was a screaming whistle sound, followed by a loud bang, and then a huge cloud of white smoke came from under the hood.

Larry stopped again, raised the hood, waited for the smoke to clear, looked around, and then turned to face us.

"I'll get you for that, Allan!" he said, and shook his fist at me. Then he got in again, and this time got off for good.

"I didn't have a thing to do with it," I said.

"You disappoint me," Keith said.

That was the last I remember talking to him. My father signaled me to return to bartending, and I spent the next hour or so passing out drinks. Marilyn helped me for a while, but I ran her off when some of Paul's friends from the vice squad began swapping stories. I don't want to sound so noble about that. Part of the reason I sent her away was because of the stories, and part of it was that I knew some of the interesting details would be sort of slipped over with her there. At the time I told myself that I sent her away too, because she was supposed to be a guest, and not an assistant bartender.

She came back about an hour later and asked me if I could take her home.

"Now, you mean?"

"No," she said. "Whenever. Later. Keith and Helen are leaving. . . ." She left it hang. She meant she wanted to stay, and that was very flattering.

"Sure," I said. She smiled at me.

"Clean up the stories, fellas," Marilyn said, raising her voice. "The lady bartender's back."

They looked a little sheepish, but they watched what they were saying. And I guess we were there together another hour, not so busy serving drinks, and more a part of the party than at first.

Then my father showed up, sort of glowing. Part of it was because it was a happy day for him, and part of it, I suspected, was because he'd had his fair share and then some of what the bar inside the house was serving.

"Can I see you a moment, Allan?" he asked, and he led me around a corner of the house. For a moment I was afraid that I was about to be told Keith had fallen off the wagon again. But it wasn't that at all.

"It seems to me," he said, "that someone as dressed up as you are, a very rare occurrence around here, shouldn't let it go to waste."

"What do you mean?"

"Well," he said, and he slipped me two twenty-dollar bills, "if I were you, I'd find a pretty girl who is also dressed to kill, and I'd take her out to dinner. I don't mean hamburgers and a coke, either. I mean a real dinner."

"What about all the food in the house?"

"We'll be eating that for the next two weeks," he said. "Go on, Allan, have a good time."

"I take it I can use your car?"

"Sure," he said, digging in his pocket for the keys. "Of course. I appreciate your filling in for the bartender," he said. "Thanks, son."

"I'm off," I said.

"Have a good time," he said, and patted me on the back like a politician.

I went back to the bar.

"What was that all about?" she asked.

"We've been pardoned," I said. "Let's get out of here."

"Where are we going?" she asked.

"Out for dinner," I said.

"Where?"

"Somewhere expensive," I said. "I am loaded."

"You don't have to do that," she said.

"Don't look my father in the mouth," I said.

"What? Oh, the gift horse?"

"Uh huh," I said.

"Okay," she said, and I could tell she was pleased.

We didn't even go through the house, we walked around the side and got in Pop's car, which he'd left parked by the curb, and drove off.

"Just between you and me," I said, "I'm glad Keith and Helen took off early."

"So am I," she said. "For a couple of reasons."

"Such as?"

"I was getting a little bored with bartending," she said.

"And?"

"It's nice to be alone with you," she said.

"Yeah."

"And something was bothering Keith," she said. "I could tell. I've known him all my life, and I can tell when he's about to blow up or cause trouble."

"Let's not even think of Keith," I said. "Okay?"

"Deal," she said.

"Where do you want to go?" I asked.

"To tell you the truth," she said, "I've been stuffing myself with shrimp and clam dip, and the rest of that stuff. And I'm not really hungry."

"So?"

"So let's go to a movie and see if we're hungry later."

"Where do you want to go? What do you want to see?"

She told me. I forget the name of the movie and the name of the actress who played in it. I'm bad about things like that. The actress is that very young one, a little girl really, fourteen, fifteen years old, and the movie was sort of a thriller. Anyway it was pretty good, and in the thriller parts Marilyn hung onto my arm or my hand, and that wasn't hard to take either. It played at Cinema Three in Livingston, and toward the end, the smell of buttered popcorn made me hungry, and when it was over and I asked Marilyn if she was hungry, she said she could eat a horse.

There's a place near Livingston called the Mushroom Farms. I'd never been in it, but I'd heard Larry and Paul talk about it. First class and expensive, they said, so I drove there.

"The prices in this place are something awful," Marilyn said, when I turned off the highway into the parking lot. "My father told me."

"Tonight I'm the last of the big spenders," I said. "Anyway, you're entitled. You were the assistant bartender."

"Why not?" she said, after that. "This is a big day, isn't it?"

The prices weren't as bad as I was afraid they would be. The bill ate a large hole in the forty bucks Pop had given me, but it was worth it. We both had the same thing, roast beef, and it was the largest piece of beef I ever saw, and delicious. Marilyn ate everything they put in front of her, from onion soup to a piece of apple pie with cheese on it for dessert.

And they had a band, two, four guys playing 1940s type music. Even that was all right. It was that kind of a place and that kind of a party, and dancing that old-fashioned way with Marilyn was a lot easier than it had been with Aunt Rose when she taught me.

CHAPTER 20

In the car on the way back to Springview, Marilyn held my hand and told me she'd had a wonderful time, the best she'd ever had.

"Let's do it again," she said. "I don't mean going to a fancy restaurant, of course. But by ourselves, without Keith and Helen wrestling in the back seat. Just you and me."

"You got it," I said.

She slid over on the seat and I put my arm around her.

And when I got to her house and walked up the walk to her door, I knew that I was going to get kissed. Really kissed. I knew she expected it.

But I didn't get to kiss her. I had just put my arms around her when the door opened, and I let go of her and found myself looking at Mr. Withers.

"Come in, please, Allan," he said, and I could tell by the tone of his voice that something was really wrong. "You have to call your father."

The first thing I thought was that something had happened to Paul. The last time I'd seen him he was reluctantly drinking coffee because he had to go on duty at half past ten.

He led me into the living room, and I dialed the number of the house.

It was busy, and I put the phone down and turned around.

"Oh, Mother, no!" Marilyn said, sort of half-screaming, half-crying, and I saw Mrs. Withers put her arms around her.

"There's been another accident, Allan," Mr. Withers said. "Helen's dead and Keith's in pretty bad shape."

I turned around and dialed the number again, and this time Paul answered on the first ring.

"Corelli," he said.

"This is Allan, Paul," I said.

"Jeez, kid, he really did it this time," Paul said. "Pop wants you to come to the Veteran's Hospital right away."

"The Veteran's Hospital?"

"It was the closest place. His girl friend, what's her name, Helen? is dead, and they're not sure about Keith."

"My God!"

"Where the hell have you been, anyway?" he said. "We've been looking all over for you."

I hung up on him.

"I've got to go to the Veteran's Hospital," I said.

"I'm going with you," Marilyn said.

"I don't think that's a very good idea, dear," her mother said.
"I'm going," Marilyn said flatly.
"We'll follow you down," Mr. Withers said. "I don't know what
we can do, but. . . ."

I don't remember that Marilyn said anything to me at all in the
fifteen minutes it took me to drive from her house to the Veteran's
Hospital in East Orange. I remember looking in the rearview
mirror once and seeing that I'd lost Mr. Withers, and thinking
that he would probably be sore about that, think that I was driving too fast and taking unnecessary chances. I wasn't, but he
would think so, and I couldn't blame him.

When I got there, I didn't know where to go, so I drove in back
where there was an "Emergency" neon sign. We parked the car
in some doctor's reserved place and half-ran toward the double-
glass doors. I remember that I didn't see any ambulances and
wondered if I had gotten the message right.

When we pushed open the glass doors, I knew I was in the right
place. Helen's mother and father were at the far end of a corridor.
Helen's mother was screaming and crying, and Helen's father and
a doctor were trying to get her to take some sort of pill. Marilyn
and I stopped, not knowing what to do. And then a nurse came
running up with a hypodermic needle. She dabbed at Helen's
mother's arm with a piece of cotton, and then stuck the needle in.

Then the four of them, Helen's parents and the doctor and the
nurse, started down the corridor. They practically had to wrestle
with Helen's mother.

Marilyn started to cry. I put my arm around her and she put
her face against me, and said, "Oh God, oh God, oh God!" Over
and over.

The doctor and the nurse didn't look at us, and Helen's mother
wasn't looking at anything at all, but her father saw us and gave

us a dirty look. I never want to get another dirty look like that as long as I live. It didn't help to tell myself that I hadn't done anything wrong. I was just glad Marilyn couldn't see it.

"That'll take effect in moments," the doctor said to Helen's father. "I suggest that you get in touch immediately with your family physician." He handed him a little bottle. "Tell him that is what we gave her. Twenty cc's."

And then they were through the glass doors and outside. I hoped that Marilyn's parents wouldn't see them, and then I realized that maybe they should. I didn't know what to think.

Then the doctor and the nurse came back in.

"Something I can do for you?" he asked.

"I'm looking for Chief Corelli," I said.

"Oh, sure. He's upstairs. Take the elevator to ten."

"Do you know what happened?" I asked.

"The story I get is the girl was running from the cops," he said. "They hit a railroad underpass."

"Oh, my God!" Marilyn said, again.

"You want to wait down here?" I asked.

"I'm going with you," she said, and put her hand on my arm, hanging on.

We got in the elevator and rode up to the tenth floor.

There were two cops there, Springview cops, and one of them was the guy who had stopped Pop when he was driving Mrs. Stevens's Mercedes. I even remembered his name: Lawton. He didn't know who I was, but he made a good guess.

"You the Chief's son?" he asked, and I nodded.

"He's in there," he said, pointing to a room with a "Lounge" sign on a frosted-glass door.

I pushed the door open. Mrs. Stevens was sitting in an armchair. Pop was sort of standing over her. She looked up at me.

"Why weren't you with him?" she said. "Why weren't you with him?"

She didn't mean, of course, that she was sorry I hadn't been in the wreck. She meant that if I had been with him, the accident probably wouldn't have happened.

"That's not fair, Virginia," my father said harshly. "That's just not fair."

"Oh, I know, I know," she said, and she started to cry again, and my father squatted beside her and awkwardly tried to put his arms around her.

"Wait outside, Allan," my father said, and we backed out of the room. I stood there for a moment, and then I walked over to Officer Lawton.

"What happened?" I asked. He looked at the other cop, who was older, and waited until the other cop nodded before replying.

"They were speeding," he said. "I started to chase them, and they started to run. And . . ." he paused, "and then she ran into the railroad underpass, the support, on South Orange Avenue. Right into it."

"Oh, boy," I said.

"They must have been drunk," he said. "There was no reason—"

"You don't know that," the older cop said. "You don't know if they were drinking or not."

"The way she was weaving . . ." he said. And I saw then that Lawton was very badly shaken up himself.

"Anyway," he went on, "the girl was dead instantly. The guy was in the back. That helped a little."

"How bad is he?"

"Pretty bad," he said. "Luckily the ambulance that answered the call had a doctor on it, an intern. He stopped most of the bleeding and brought him here. That probably saved his life."

"Is he going to live?" Marilyn asked. Her voice was faint, but she was in control of herself.

"I don't know, miss," Officer Lawton said. "They're working on him now."

Keith lived. But that's not the same thing as saying he recovered. He was all right, mentally, I mean, for a couple of days after the accident. He told us what had happened. After Howell had told him that he would have to go back to court that next week, he just had to have a drink. And so I wouldn't see him drinking at Larry's and Barbara's reception, he left. Helen drove. They went to Ernie's, and Helen sat there with him, feeling sorry for him because she knew how much he hated the idea of going back to court. And he got bombed. What he didn't expect was that Helen, who didn't have nearly as much to drink as he did, wasn't used to it or couldn't handle it as well, and she got drunk, too.

So when they finally drove home, Lawton had seen her weaving and turned the bubble-gum machine on to stop them, and it seemed like a good idea to run for it. He didn't want Helen to get arrested for drunken driving.

Keith wasn't trying to put the blame on Helen. He accepted full responsibility. It was all his fault. And that was enough to push him over the edge. He just couldn't take it. He flipped.

They've got him in a private mental hospital in New Haven, Connecticut. He doesn't rant and rave and act crazy, according to my father, who goes up there every other week with Mrs. Stevens, to see him. He just sits and stares at the floor. Sometimes he recognizes his mother and Pop and sometimes he doesn't. Pop said the psychiatrists told him that what he had done, what he thought he had done, was just too much for him. He's retreated inside himself, because he can't face reality. Pop told me that maybe he was a little unstable before the accident, but that what had happened to him could happen to anybody.

They say they hope he'll come out of it in time, but they're not making any promises, or even suggesting when this might happen. All we can do is wait.

And, oh yeah, the day after we buried Helen, they tried Mr. Waldron again. They found him guilty this time, and the judge fined him $250 and suspended his license for six months. He's appealing.